Fallin' In Love With The Goat 2

By: Tiece

Text Tiece to 42828 to sign up for Email Alerts

By: Tiece

Recap

"Damn man, you whooped Pooler's ass like he was a newborn baby." Slick exclaimed in an excited tone. "Took that nigga's pink slip right from under his nose."

Jabari grinned. "Hell yea, I did that. I knew he was going down. It was no way around it."

"Boy I feel like I won the race, that's how powerful that shit was. I knew it was on when you tossed your coin in the air and that bitch landed on heads. I knew then, that's his ass!"

"I did too," Jabari smugly chuckled, as he turned up his red plastic cup filled with Patron and orange juice. "That was one of the most exciting races I've ever had. It was even better than the races I had with Ace. The crowd was hype and people was chanting my name, shit was real tonight."

He said, feeling very proud of himself.

"You had niggas out there jumping up and down, hollin' and shit. It was a wild night."

Jabari smiled, as he glanced down at his cell phone chirping of an incoming text message. He saw that it was Cashmere, but continued talking to Slick.

"He didn't wanna give up the pink slip to that nice ass Chevelle S.S."

"That hoe got a 540 big block in it too. He just don't know how to drive the bitch."

"I agree, but I'm gon' stunt on that nigga. We gon' be racing his shit. Show 'em how it's done."

"That's right." Slick said, as he drove in the direction of his house. He looked over at his Jabari with a proud smile on his face. "I'm happy for you, man."

"Preciate that Bruh." Jabari said, as his phone chirped again.

Again, he glanced down at it and then continued his conversation with Slick. "So, what's been going on with you?" he pondered. "You ain't been hanging around like you normally do. You a'ight?"

"Yea, Bruh. I'm good. You remember when I went to California a year ago?"

"Yea."

"Well, I ran into this dude that knew of your family. He told me he followed your father's career back when he was racing. He even knew of Papers."

"Who don't know Papers?" Jabari grinned. "Especially if they know Pops."

"You right," Slick laughed. "But, this dude also mentioned some strange shit that kind of went over my head, back then. But a few months back, I stumbled across something that bothered me and got me to thinking a lil deeper about what dude said. I've been just been laying low, kind of on the prowl."

"Just tell me, even it ain't true. I need to know what you're talking about."

"Calm down, Bruh. The only thing you need to be doing is finding a bed to take yo' drunk ass to sleep in." Slick chuckled.

"Nigga I'm good." Jabari shot his way with a slight smile.

"Listen, don't worry. I'm gonna meet up with him later and just talk to him. At least that's the plan."

Jabari glanced down at his watch. "It's already 2 in the morning. Who you meeting up with and why?"

"If I bring something to you I'm first gon' make sure it's solid shit; especially this shit. Me and this nigga pretty cool, though. It won't be no smoke, I promise you. But if I find out it's true it will be—"

"So, it's involving us? Me?" Jabari cut in.

"Not per say you, but it's close to home. I just hope it ain't true. But look, I'll tell you all about it when you and Cain come by. We still hittin' up the court in the morning, right?"

"You know we always have to get a good game in after we have a big race. We've done that since I could remember. Ain't nothing changed. Plus, I love dunking on you and Cain's ass. I believe Justin is gonna join us in the morning too. I'm spanking er'body's ass." He joked, turning up his celebratory drink.

"If yo' ass can make it." Slick laughed. "You going over to Cashmere's?"

"Nah, she keep texting me, but I ain't going over there. I'll probably take my ass on home after you get out."

"Nigga, you sho' you can drive home?"

"Yea, I got this." Jabari said. "I drive better drunk."

Slick laughed. "Yea, whatever."

"I saw Cashmere exchanging numbers with Pooler tonight." He blurted out of nowhere.

"Huh? When you saw that?"

"After the race." He answered, with a disappointed shake of the head.

"Why the fuck would she wanna talk to a loser?" he teased, but was very serious. "You sure you saw that?"

"What I saw was her with her phone out and him with his out. He made a call from his phone and she clicked hers and then typed something in it. I ain't crazy. That nigga called her phone and she saved his number."

"Damn, if you peeped all that from wherever you were at, it must've been meant for you to see it."

"Yea, I be trying with shawty but it be the slick shit she do that makes me not trust her. Technically, I know we not together, but I still be going over every now and then." He said. "Shit, I still look out and even as of lately." He added.

"Yea, I feel you, but maybe you should holla at her. She keeps texting you." He said, glancing down at Jabari's cell phone. "Get her side of the story before you just spazz out on her." Slick advised, as he pulled up in his driveway.

"You sho' you wanna meet a nigga this time of night?" he asked, ignoring Slick's unadvised comments. "I can stick around if you need me to." He added.

"It's all good Bruh. I know him." Slick assured him. "Plus, I'm just gon' feel him out. I ain't gon' even say much about it, but I do think he's the same nigga I think spreading lies about me. And if that part is true, then no telling what else is true."

"Damn, that sounds serious though."

"It is, but it ain't no big deal tonight. So, don't worry yourself. He just coming over for some work. We do business round this time of the morning anyway. You know this strip is like Vegas. It's always hot."

"Which is the main reason why I stayed for a few days and then hauled ass. I don't like all that damn traffic."

Slick laughed.

"It ain't that bad."

"You was the one that said it was hot nigga." He laughed.

"Well, yea but I was just fucking around."

"No, you weren't." Jabari chimed in causing Slick to laugh.

"Anyway," Slick said, as he opened the car door. "Talk to Cashmere. Don't just leave her hanging."

"You've become one of her biggest fans, I see. Ever since she cried on your shoulder, you got a lil soft spot for her."

"Only because I do believe the girl likes you. Regardless of what she did or didn't do, she still loves you."

"I can believe that." Jabari said. "But, sometimes love just ain't enough."

Slick shrugged.

"I feel you." He said, getting out the car, so Jabari could take the wheel.

"Be careful Bruh. I'll text you when I get up in the morning." Jabari said, just as his phone chirped of another text message.

"Text the woman back." Slick grinned, as he headed up on his porch. "I insist!"

Jabari glanced down at his cell phone.

"I'll text her back, since you insist." He grinned.

Fifteen minutes later, Jabari found himself tapping on the front door. "Damn, I can't believe I'm here." He mumbled, followed by knocking lightly once more. The door opened and a smile spread across his face.

"You made it," Tiana said, smiling just as big as he was.

"Yea, I did. Can't believe you actually hit me up this time of morning."

"I couldn't get you off my mind. Come in." She told him.

Jabari didn't waste any time walking in the house behind Tiana. She had the soultry sounds of Ella Mai playing on the surround sound throughout the house.

"Your spot is nice."

"Thanks," she said. "You want something to drink? A beer or something?" she asked.

"Yea, let me get a beer." He said. He was already lit, but he figured the beer might calm his liquor down some. He watched Tiana as her fat ass jiggled in a pair of red boy shorts she was walking around in. "Damn, she fine." He whispered to himself.

Tiana returned with a Bud Light and handed it to him. Jabari didn't care what kind of beer it was, he just wanted something to drink.

"Come on," she said.

"Where we going? You ain't tryna kidnap me are you?"

"Maybe, so if you can't stay the rest of the night then it might be in your best interest to leave now." She teased, but had a serious expression on her face.

"Shiiiiiiiid, I'm staying the night. I ain't going nowhere." Jabari clowned, but was very serious.

Tiana laughed. "Well, follow me." She said, leading him to her bedroom.

Jabari walked in and looked around the room. It was a room inside a room. The smaller section of the room was used as Tiana's office space. It had a clear desk, a circular chair with a big plush pillow in it, and a few motivational pictures hanging on the wall. A big, California King bed was centered in the other part of the room and off to the side of it was a loveseat. On the wall was a big screen TV. Jabari approvingly nodded his head. He liked her space. It was comfortable and cozy."

"Sit down anywhere you want."

"What if I wanna lay on the bed?"

"In that case, lay anywhere you want." She told him with a cute smile.

Jabari sat his beer on a coaster that was on the dresser. He came out of his shoes and did just that, as he laid across the foot of her bed.

"Let me help you come out the rest of your stuff." She said, getting up on the big bed, and straddling him. As she helped Jabari come out of his shirt, he started planting sweet kisses around her neck. Tiana's head rolled back, enjoying his touch. He pulled her fitted tank top over her head and palmed her breasts with his hands. He tongue played from one nipple to the other, causing an arousal in Tiana that she'd been looking forward to for a while.

She moaned softly in his ear and then he flipped her over so he could be on top. He slipped out of his pants so smooth she didn't even know they were off until she felt his erection pushing through his boxer briefs.

Damn, she thought.

Jabari passionately sucked Tiana's breasts. Her body was definitely saying yes. He could feel her squirming inside, but this was just the warm-up. He was about to give her an overdose of vitamin D; a lifetime prescription she could get anytime she needed it. She had no clue what she was in for. He stopped himself, before he switched gears because once that happened it was no turning back.

"You sure you wanna do this?" he asked.

Tiana smiled. "You sure you wanna do this?"

"Hell yea," he responded.

"Say less then," she told him, as she leaned towards him. She kissed him on the lips and started helping him come out of her red boy shorts. It was definitely about to go down.

He reached over on the bed, where he'd taken his condoms out his pocket and grabbed one. He slipped it on and then laid his warm, naked body on top of hers. She wrapped her thick thighs around his waist. "I like that," he whispered, while playing with the juicy entrance of her temple. He slid in with ease, as her creamy walls gripped his pipe. A few pumps in and he knew he had struck gold. Her gushy insides had him stroking like he wanted to go half on a baby. Luckily, he had on his safety net.

After giving her a serious smack down for nearly thirty-minutes, he paused and pulled out to put on a new condom. "Turn over," he told her. Tiana wasted no time succumbing to his wants and desires, as she backed her ass up on him.

"Like that?"

"Just like that." He told her, while rubbing his dick against her fat, salacious lips. He backed up a little to take it all in. This was a moment he had wished a many of times he could be in. Intoxicated and gone off that Patron had him turned up. His sex drive was on 100 and he had the rest of the night to prove just how bad he wanted her.

The minute he slid in from the back, she started backing it up on him, winding on it and bouncing her ass up and down on it. He tried standing up in it, but a tidal wave of cream filled juices squirted out, causing him to stop for a minute to gain his composure. "Damn girl," he whispered.

"You lay down." She told him.

Jabari did as he was asked and laid back on the bed. Tiana straddled him with her thick thighs wrapped around his sexy frame. She slid down covering his long wood, and then took in a deep breath from the amazing feeling it gave her. Her walls were sensitive, causing her insides to spill over as she rode him from the front and then from the back. High as a kite and gone off that Tito, she could go for hours. Pussy was poppin' all over the place, as he carried her in his arms and fucked her against the wall. From the wall to her desk, bending her over and consistently hitting it from the back.

Two hours in and they had touched every piece of furniture in her room. He made his way to the loveseat, as Tiana followed him. Once again getting on top, she had plans this time and wasn't going to move until he bust one. She eased down on the crown of his head, making her walls grip his dick as it slid in deeper.

"Damn," he let out.

Tiana stayed focused, and bounced up and down, fast then slow like she was on a bull at a rodeo. She closed her eyes, feeling a tingling sensation rush over her body. She stared him in the eyes, and then kissed him softly on the lips. "I'm cummin' Jah." She whispered.

"Me too," he whispered back, squeezing her butt cheeks with both hands, and then wasting no more time, as he painted the inside of her walls white. "Damn, I'm sorry 'bout that. You on something?"

"No, but you're good." She told him. "I'm not ovulating."

"You sure? I didn't know I was gonna go through four condoms."

"It's cool. You're good." She assured him.

"Okay," he said, as he laid back on the sofa like he was out of breath and sleepy as hell.

"Come, get in the bed." Tiana insisted, as she escorted Jabari to the bed. In no time, he was lightly snoring. He cupped his arm around her waist, and she fell asleep with a smile on her face.

The next morning, Jabari woke up and glanced over at Tiana. She was still sound asleep, snoring and all. He grinned to himself while being in a blissful state. He couldn't believe that it had finally gone down after all those years of wanting this to happen. It couldn't have happened at a more perfect time. Not only did he win the pink slip to a rival's car, but he hit the lotto just by waking up in Tiana's bed.

This shit gotta be a dream, he jokingly thought. As he lay there, he reminisced about being in a good space with a good girl. Tiana was somebody he could see himself being with. Even though he wasn't going to push the envelope, it was still a thought he'd keep near and dear. Cashmere crossed his mind, but only briefly. After the connection he and Tiana had made, he figured it would be best to stop fucking Cashmere. It was no longer a need to drag it out when he felt in his heart that it was really over.

As he lay there, his cell phone chirped of an incoming text message. He picked his phone up off the nightstand. He saw a few missed messages from Cain and a lot of missed messages from Cashmere. Trying to check Cain's text first, his finger slipped and hit Cashmere's message instead. The last thing she text him showed first.

I've been hitting you all morning trying to tell you something. I don't know what your problem is. I thought we were good. CASHMERE

Yea, we were good until you fucked up. He thought as he continued to read the rest of the message.

I've been sick and didn't know why. Well, I took a test and it came back positive. I'm pregnant with your baby. Call me when you get this message. We really need to talk. CASHMERE

Jabari frowned with a confused look on his face. *Did she just say she's pregnant?* He asked himself. *I know better.*

His thoughts went from being mad at her to now not knowing how to feel. Was she really pregnant or playing tricks on him? After all, another shawty had just played that same game with Slick. He looked over at Tiana. If it was true, this couldn't have come at a worse time. How could he possibly be planning to move on with somebody else, if Cashmere was pregnant? His heart wouldn't let him play it that raw. He would have no choice but to give her a chance for the sake of their baby. He sighed with an annoyed shake of the head. Nothing could get as bad as this. *FUUUUCK!* He screamed in his mind, just as his cell phone rang. He glanced down at the display screen and let out a sigh of relief when he noticed it was Cain calling and not Cashmere.

"Damn, I'm late," he whispered, as he noticed the time. He jumped up out of bed, so he could wash up. "Wassup Bruh?" he answered, while finding his clothes strewed about the floor. "I'll be heading that way shortly."

"I've been texting you for the past forty minutes."

"My bad, I got caught up and I'm just waking up." He grinned like his playboy status was on a thousand. "I'm coming."

"Hold up, don't leave yet. You may wanna even sit down for this." Cain said, in a nervous tone.

"What's wrong Bruh? You good?"

"Nah, I ain't good?" he whimpered in the phone.

Jabari instantly knew something wasn't right. He could hear his brother choking up like he couldn't get his words out. "Bruh, you scaring me."

Silence could be heard on the other end. It was like Cain's whole voice had disappeared.

"Cain? Bruh?! YOU A'IGHT?!" Jabari asked even louder in the phone. His voice rose so high he woke up Tiana.

"Jah, this Justin."

"What's going on with Cain? Talk to me, Bruh." Jabari said with worried eyes and a concerned tone.

Me and Cain over here to Slick's house. He's gone man. He's gone." Justin cried through trembled words.

"Gone?! What you mean he's gone?"

Justin took in a deep breath and then let it out. "Somebody shot and killed him. He's gone."

By: Tiece

Chapter One

"You good, B?" Cain asked as he stepped outside of the shop to find his brother sitting alone and staring off into space.

"Nah, I got a lot on my mind." He responded with a shake of the head. "It's too much going on, and I'm trying not to lose it."

"You can't lose it, Bruh. You gotta keep it together."

"I know, but it's hard." He said in a saddened, angry tone. "Some bitch ass nigga out here running around a free man and we still don't have a clue who it is. It's almost 2 weeks later, and still nobody's talking. What the fuck?!" he angrily yelled.

"Calm down, B. Calm down." Cain said, as he walked over to console his brother. "You've been taking this thing really hard and I can understand why, but you can't let it consume you. I don't even understand what's going on and why the truth hasn't come to light, but you gotta fall back. Let Pops and Unc do what they do best. They'll find out who did it and when they do—"

"They better kill 'em. Whoever the nigga is." Jabari heatedly cut in.

"You already know how it's going down. Right now, we should all be laying low. All of this could have something to do with me getting shot that night."

"Grazed," Jabari uttered with a shake of the head.

Cain frowned. "What? What'd you say?"

"I said grazed, Bruh. You got grazed by a bullet not shot."

Cain shot him the side-eye. "Yea, whatever." He continued. "It could've had something to do with him owing a nigga on the streets."

"Nah, I talked with him about that and he said he didn't owe nobody. I believed him. He wasn't lying about it. This shit is deeper than we think it is and it's close to home."

"Why you say that?"

"Because he had talked to me about some shit he'd been looking into."

"What shit?" Cain pondered with a clueless expression. "What was going on?"

"I don't know. He didn't go into full details. He only said he stumbled on some information back when he had gone to California, some shit he found out on a whim. Ironically, what he heard was something that supposedly hits close to home for us."

"Close to home for who?"

"For us, as in we, as in the McCoy's." he explained.

Cain sat quietly for a moment. "And he had this talk with you the night he got killed?"

"Yea, and he also said he was meeting with somebody he served that night to see if he could find out some answers, but he assured me that everything was cool."

"So, this guy is someone we know?"

"Yea."

"Why you ain't been said something about this?"

"I don't know, Bruh. I've just been thinking and trying to figure this shit out."

"You should've told Pops, at least."

"I will." Jabari told him, as he then sat in silence for a minute. "I asked him if he wanted me to stay with him that night, but he said no. I had this gut feeling, but I didn't know what to make of it. Till this day I regret not staying."

"You shouldn't, it's not your fault. Plus, had you been there and not knowing what was going on, it could've been worse. It was meant for you to leave."

"But meant for him to die? That ain't right." He mumbled with a sad shake of the head.

"I'm just saying B. Life ain't fair. We know that. Pops is already 'round here on edge. Losing Slick was like losing a son for him and a nephew for Unc. It took us back to losing Skylar so unexpectedly. We're all going through it. Slick was like a brother to us and a son to Mama."

"I know, and that's why I'm so sick man. I can't shake this shit. It's been almost a week since we buried him, but it feels like it was just yesterday. The main thing that bothered me was how his mama put on. She only showed out like that because he won't be around to make sure she's good. I never understood the relationship she had with him. She was the child and he was the parent."

"Yea, they did have a strange relationship. He had been taking care of her since he was about twelve years old. I know we grew up in the fast lane, but he grew up fast. There's a difference."

"You right about that." Jabari agreed.

"What y'all out here talking about?" Justin asked, as he exited the shop doors.

"We're just talking about Slick." Cain responded.

"Slick wouldn't won't us to be down and out. He would want us to keep living." Justin told them.

"That's hard to do when we don't know what really happened to him." Jabari uttered.

"And, that's not something we should worry about. The truth will come to the light. Pops and Unc are on it." Justin relayed.

Jabari sighed. "Yea, but they ain't came up with nothing yet."

"Nothing that you can see, but for the most part they're low-key asking around. You know how they operate. It may take some time." Justin said.

"The longer the time the deeper this shit is. That's why they need to hurry up." Cain cut in, now starting to feel where his brother was coming from.

"And, that's all I'm saying," Jabari agreed.

"Well, today is not the day to be dwelling on this subject. You have a race this weekend and Pops wanna do a few tests runs later. So, you need to clear your thoughts and get your head back in the game."

"He's right," Cain agreed.

"I know," Jabari said with a nod of the head. "It's just hard."

"It is," Cain uttered, as a moment of silence crept in. The brothers were caught up in their thoughts and feeling blue over losing another person that was near and dear to their hearts. Cain looked up and said a short prayer to himself, and then let out a hopeful sigh. The sky hovering above was just as cloudy as his mental, indicating rainfall soon. He glanced back over at Jabari, wanting so bad for him to be okay. Not only that, but he prayed that God would keep him safe; that he'd keep all of them safe.

Jabari took in a deep breath and then let it out. Briefly, he looked over at Cain, and then Justin, as he decided to share another secret he'd been keeping. "Cashmere is pregnant."

Cain frowned. "What? Say what now?"

"I said that Cashmere is pregnant."

"Damn, Bruh." Justin said. "I wanna say congratulations, but from the look on your face—"

"Right, because I don't know if it's mine." He admitted.

"Wow, why would you say that?" Cain pondered. "I mean, I know y'all split, but you have been sliding through there right?"

"Yea, but I just always had a feeling that Cash was doing something behind my back. So, for us to be broken up and she hits me with this—"

"Makes you feel some type of way." Cain cut in.

"Exactly." Jabari responded with a regrettable shake of the head. "I should be happy, at least about that, but I can't be. I'm so fucking confused right now. I know she loves me, but shawty has a side that I been peeped a long time ago. She has this fetish when it comes to sex and in getting what she wants. So, when I got locked up, I couldn't shake knowing that she might be fucking around for her own selfish needs. Whether it was for sex or for money."

Cain and Justin shook their heads. They really didn't know what to say. Jabari had already mentioned not trusting Cashmere, but they didn't know it was that deep.

"The only thing I can tell you, Bruh is to get a DNA test done. That way you'll know for sure." Cain slid in.

"Yea, but what am I supposed to do now? I don't wanna neglect her and then end up being the father of the baby. I'll feel bad as hell. But, what if I go all in, and then find out it's not?"

"That's all a part of life, B. You just gotta follow your heart. Do what it tells you to do. You'll know if it's the right thing or not." Justin told him.

"Yea, but that's easier said than done."

"I can believe it." Cain mumbled. "I can't lie though. I hated not being there for mine. I had my own selfish reasons, but I wish now I could turn back the hands of time. I'm already in a bind where I can't even see 'em unless I go to them. They don't know me like that, so the mama's aren't letting them come over. The last time that happened, Lauren and Sofia got into so bad that she ain't trying to hear shit about Cannon coming back no time soon. On top of that, Lauren ain't feeling me going to see them, either. She don't care about the babies coming to my place, but she ain't with me going to theirs. So, I'm just fucked up any way you look at it."

"Damn Bruh, I didn't know it was that bad." Jabari said.

"Hell yea, I can't seem to catch a fucking break." Cain irritably said. "Lauren acts like it's cool, because she knows how important this is for me. But I can tell it breaks her heart. I don't know what to do about it. I don't wanna keep hurting her over and over again, but I don't wanna let her go. She's a good woman. It would kill me to see her move on with another nigga."

"I feel you." Jabari uttered.

"But my heart is telling me that I gotta get to know my kids. It's important that they know me and know that I got them no matter what. Pops always made sure we was good. Even when Jabari was born and him and Mama went their separate ways for a couple of years, we didn't feel that shit. He still came around. He still made sure we knew he was there."

"You right, because I never knew they weren't together. For as long as I can remember, Pops has always been there."

"That's because she took him back around the time you turned two or three. Being that you're 6 years younger than me, you wouldn't have remembered any of that, anyway."

"Yea, I know. But, like you said, he was always around. I guess I'll just keep praying about it. At some point I gotta talk to Cash, though."

"So, when did she tell you she was pregnant?" Justin pondered.

"The same morning y'all called to tell me about Slick." He answered.

"Damn, that wasn't the best of timing." Justin said.

"Same thing I was thinking." Cain chimed in. "It's been 2 weeks since that happened. I do think it's time you talk to her. You don't wanna leave her hanging too long. They start acting crazy when you do that." He advised, just as Lauren and Tiana drove up.

Jabari glanced up at the car coming their way. He smiled at just the thought of seeing Tiana. For some reason, she always made him feel better.

"I can't believe that Lauren is still working here. I thought that would only be temporary." Justin grinned.

"Me too," Cain uttered. "I guess that's one way of her watching me and making sure I'm where I supposed to be."

"I guess," Jabari mumbled.

"So, what's up with you and Tiana?" Justin asked.

"Nothing," Jabari answered. "We just cool." He and Tiana had already decided that they wouldn't tell nobody about the amazing night they shared. Unfortunately, it had only happened once. It had been so much going on that he didn't have the time or the need for it. Now wasn't the time to go all in with someone new when he still had shit going on with someone old.

Cain grinned. "Okay, if you say so. But the way y'all act around each other is saying something different."

"We don't even see each other like that." Jabari shot his way.

"So, you say," Cain teased as Justin laughed.

Jabari shook his head. "Chill Bruh, they getting out the car now."

"I'll chill this time." Cain joked. "But, I know y'all got something going on."

"Nah," Jabari grinned.

"Wassup y'all?" Lauren spoke, as she handed Cain a Wendy's bag. "Jah, if I knew you were going to be here I would've gotten you some lunch too."

"Oh, nah, I'm good." Jabari responded.

"Hey B," Tiana spoke with a smile, as she walked over and sat down beside him.

"Wassup up pretty lady?" He spoke back. Neither had mentioned a thing about them messing around, so they played their cards carefully when in the presence of others.

"Nothing much. Lauren and I went out to lunch. She actually treated today," she jokingly answered.

"You act like I don't never treat." Lauren cut in.

"You don't," Tiana told her, as everyone laughed. "So, you alright?" she asked while turning her attention back to Jabari. Their conversations had somewhat been on the backburner due to Slick's death. She missed Jabari, but she played it cool in not wanting him to know how bad.

"I don't have a choice but to be." He told her with a slight smile. He glanced back to see that Justin, Cain and Lauren were off in their own conversation, joking around about something. So, he took the opportunity to shoot a small shot her way. "I've been thinking about you heavy. I ain't gon' lie. I miss you."

Tiana blushed with a sincere smile. "I've missed you too."

"I don't want you to think I don't want you, because damn I do. But, it's been crazy, and I've been taking time to get my mind wrapped around everything that's going on. I do want you so bad. I just don't wanna bring no negative energy in your space."

"You could never do that." Tiana assured him. "So, maybe we can link later and talk. I think talking will help you ease some of that tension. You know, I'm pretty good with my hands. I can give you the best massage you've never had." She joked, as she glanced back to make sure that the others weren't paying attention to them.

"That's the best thing I've heard all day." Jabari responded just as Cashmere's car was seen driving up the gravel paveway. "What the fuck she doing here?" he pondered with a frown on his face.

"Ah shit, I hope she ain't on nothing crazy." Cain chimed in, as everybody looked to see who was invading their territory.

"She better not be unless she wanna get that ass beat today." Lauren cut in with a roll of the eyes. "What the hell you did to her Jah? That bitch crazy."

Jabari simply shook his head. He glanced over at Tiana. "This might get a lil interesting. You can go inside the shop if you want to."

"You want me to go in there?" Tiana asked.

"That's up to you. Either way, she shouldn't be coming here to start no shit. I ain't gon' let her touch you even if she tried, anyway."

"Well, say less. I'm staying." Tiana told him.

By: Tiece

Chapter Two

Cashmere parked her car directly in front of where Jabari and Tiana were sitting.

"Girl, don't get out here showing yo' ass." Shyla uttered.

"I'm tired of this nigga." Cashmere responded, as she got out of the car. Shyla jumped out, too. She was more so trying to keep up with Cashmere, as she made her way right over to Jabari.

"So, you can't call nobody now? You can't come over and talk to me? I feel bad about Slick's death too, so you can't keep using that as an excuse."

Jabari irritably shook his head. He didn't get up, but he eyed Cashmere up and down before responding. "Are you crazy? Why are you here; you following me or something?"

"You heard what I asked you. What is your problem?" she asked now looking over at Tiana. "Is this your problem? Is she the reason why you're acting funny? I saw her all in your face at the funeral."

Tiana grinned while standing to her feet. "This might get ugly, so I'm gonna head into the shop." She said, as she attempted to walk off, but was stopped by Cashmere's hand pulling her back by the arm.

Tiana shot Cashmere a side-eye. "If you don't get your paws off me, I know something."

"I'm just saying—"

"You just saying what, Cashmere? Cause you ain't gon' do this, not here, not ever." Jabari firmly told her, as he stood up to get between the two women.

"Why the fuck she always gotta show up acting stupid?" Lauren cut in, clearly with an attitude. "Bitch act like y'all together or something."

"Bitch?! I got yo' bitch, BITCH!"

"Wait a minute!!" Cain jumped in to try and hold Lauren back.

"I'll drag yo' ass." Lauren told her, trying to break free from Cain's grip.

"Hold up, it ain't gon' be no dragging 'round here." Shyla jumped in, and without saying another word she quickly swung on Lauren. Justin grabbed her from behind trying to hold her back.

"Ayyyyyyeee!! Don't y'all do this!!" Justin yelled out.

Tiana was now trying to get to Cashmere with Jabari in between the two trying to stop them from tearing each other a part. Jabari was trying to hold Tiana back, which only pissed Cashmere off more because it seemed like he was protecting Tiana over her.

Justin had picked Shyla up and was carrying her across his shoulder back to the car. He opened the door and sat her in it like she was a child. "Listen, ma. You can't be doing this at my Pop's place of business. The shit ain't lady-like." He told her.

"Move, so I can get my cousin." Shyla told him.

"No, cause you tripping. Both of y'all tripping and dead ass wrong." He said with a serious expression.

"I don't care. Can you move?"

"No," Justin told her. "B, you need help?" he called out.

"Nah, I'm good." He responded after calming Tiana down. It left no choice but for Cashmere to calm down, since she couldn't act a fool by herself.

"So, it's like this?" Cashmere asked with a confused, disappointed, and saddened expression all rolled in one. She held her stomach like suddenly remembering she was pregnant. "It's obvious you want her." She spat.

"You wouldn't be making accusations if you weren't always popping up thinking shit." Jabari told her. "Plus, we aren't together." He added.

"So, you DON'T want her?" Cashmere pondered, as she stared in his eyes waiting for an indication that would tell her if he did.

Jabari stood there not knowing what to say being that Tiana hadn't fully walked off, yet.

"Well?" Cashmere asked, as she looked from Tiana and then back to Jabari. "You don't want her? Tell me. Tell me what the deal is now."

"The only thing I'm telling you is that it's past time for you to leave." He responded.

"Bitch! You heard him. LEAVE!" Lauren yelled out.

"Hush," Cain said, as he covered her mouth. "This ain't got nothing to do with you."

"If my sister involved, so am I."

Jabari shook his head. It was too much shit going on for him. "Cashmere, it's time for you to leave." He told her again, but in a much more demanding tone.

"Okay, I'll leave, but did he tell you that we're pregnant?"

Tiana's eyes widened.

"YOU'RE pregnant." Jabari corrected her.

"Oh, so now you're denying your baby?" Cashmere asked, as Tiana shook her head and simply walked off. She'd had enough.

By: Tiece

"Come on, Sis. Let's go in the shop. You ain't gotta leave because this bitch out here acting a fool."

"If I wasn't pregnant I would beat yo' ass." Cashmere told Lauren.

"Come on bitch. Try me today! I hate to say it Jah, but I would beat that baby right out of her ass!" Lauren yelled out.

"Maaaannn," Cain uttered, as he grabbed Lauren and headed inside of the shop.

"I'm outta here." Tiana said, as she headed for her car.

Jabari wanted to stop her, because he hadn't mentioned the baby, but instead he let her be. It was no use explaining the situation when tensions were already heated.

Tiana got in her car and wasted no time leaving the scene.

"You really like that bitch, don't you?" Cashmere asked. She noticed how time seemed to have stopped as Jabari watched Tiana leave.

"You really pissing me off. You got 2 seconds to get in yo' car and leave." Jabari calmly said, but the serious look on his face told Cashmere that he wasn't with the bullshit no more.

"Okay, cool. If you don't wanna talk now, don't think we're talking later." She told him. "We don't need you."

Jabari shrugged his shoulders while standing his ground. What he'd said was definitely understood, as Cashmere got in her car.

"I told you not to come out here." Shyla eased in. She was now embarrassed that the whole thing had occurred.

"Man, fuck them!" Cashmere shouted. "You'll regret this day!" She told Jabari, as he started walking towards her car. Cashmere quickly put the car in reverse. Apparently, she didn't want no smoke, because she could tell that Jabari wasn't walking out there to be nice. In no time, she was clearing the path as she hauled ass out of there.

"Damn Bruh, you a'ight?" Justin asked with a shake of the head.

"Yea, Bruh. Tell Pops I'll be back. I gotta clear my head." He responded, and with that, he got in his car and peeled out too.

Cashmere laid across the bed with tears coming down her face. "Shyla I'm so sick. I don't know what to do with myself."

"I know," Shyla responded, as she attempted to comfort her bestie.

"I can't stop crying. Hell, I'm in my feelings about Jabari and Slick. How is that even possible? Every time I think about either of them I get sad all over again; especially knowing that Slick is gone forever now."

"I think it was a shock to the whole community. Slick was a cool cat. Yea, he had some shady ass ways for y'all to have been fucking behind Jabari's back, but still. He wasn't a bad person and definitely not that bad of a person to go out like that."

"I know right," Cashmere whispered. "On top of that, Jabari is acting like a real dick. He won't talk to me and the shit got me losing my damn mind."

"Jabari has a lot going on. He lost his best friend."

Cashmere sighed. "I get that, but he still shouldn't be that way. Slick is gone. God rest his soul. We all have to keep living which means that Jabari still needs to be here for me at a time like this. I'm just hurt that he's not. He won't even let me be there for him. Every time I reach out, he's mostly alone at his crib, or so he says. To make matters worse, he hasn't even extended an invite for me to visit him."

"You gotta give the man time."

"If he let me in then maybe I can help him ease the pain of losing Slick."

"I think it's a bit deeper than that. They were all sick as hell. Did you see them at that funeral? I ain't never seen that many niggas in one place breaking down like that. Cain and Jabari were the only two really trying to hold up, but even Jabari broke down once. Poor Justin, Papers had to walk him out. Every nigga in there shed a tear for Slick. That shit was sad as hell. Not a dry eye in the building."

"That's how you know he was loved. But, enough about Slick," Cashmere uttered, not wanting to dive back into those feelings. "I just can't believe Jabari did me like that in front of another bitch. What was he thinking?"

"Cash, I don't think it happened the way it looked, if that makes sense."

Cashmere frowned. "Don't make no damn sense to me. Elaborate please," she added.

"Well, technically you were the one that showed up acting a fool. You know Jabari doesn't like that. He never has. So, for him to seemingly be on her side, just meant that he wasn't taking yours because of how you confronted him."

"I don't give a fuck. I'm the one that's pregnant with his baby. He should've taken my side regardless. Or, at least given me the time of day. He could've walked off with me or something."

"Nah, I highly doubt that would've happened. You got out the car talking reckless."

"Right now ain't the time to be taking up for his ass. You can get up and leave." Cashmere bluntly advised. "I ain't with this shit. I'm sitting here pregnant, in my feelings about Slick's death too, and Jabari won't fuck with me. Yet, you got the nerve to be taking sides? Oh, hell no!"

"Girl calm down. You're so damn dramatic. You know I have your back, but I'm also gonna keep it one thousand."

"Yea, but I don't need your one thousand, one hundred, or two cents. You can keep all that." Cashmere explained with an irritated shake of the head.

"Okay, I get it. You're hurt and I'm hurt too just to see you feeling down like this, especially with you being pregnant."

"What?" Cashmere questioned, after looking at the serious expression on Shyla's face.

"Is that baby Jabari's? You know you can tell me. I won't say nothing."

Cashmere just stared at her. She didn't say a word at first, while thinking, *I know this bitch ain't trying me.* "Guess you can't take my word for it either, huh? Just get out my house."

Shyla frowned. "You can't be serious."

"I'm dead serious."

"Well, you ain't gotta be acting like that, but I'll leave." Shyla said, as she stood to her feet. "You shouldn't be acting like this. I just asked a simple question. Don't act like it's not a relevant one."

"The only thing that's relevant right now is you getting yo' ass outta my house." Cashmere fussed. "If this baby wasn't Jabari's you would've been the first to know. It ain't like I don't tell you everything."

"Well, I didn't know. I just wanted to make sure. You could've been saying that you were pregnant to make it work. I can't judge you for that, because I know how much you want him back in your life."

"Yea, but even if that were true you'd be talking shit saying that I was wrong and should be honest with him."

"Well—"

"Well my ass. Let me walk you out." Cashmere said, as she stood to her feet to walk Shyla out.

"That baby already got yo' ass acting crazy as fuck." Shyla uttered. "I hope I don't have to put up with this stank ass attitude for the whole 9 months."

"Who knows? You just might." She said, as she made her way to the front door. When she opened it, she gasped for air while holding her chest. "Dirty! What the fuck? You scared me."

"My bad. I was 'bout to knock." He said. "Wassup? You had messaged me the day before yesterday wanting something to smoke but I was still out of town. I just wanted to drop this off."

"Come on in, Dirty." Shyla said from behind.

"How you gon' invite somebody in, but you're leaving?"

"Oh, I ain't going nowhere now. Dirty is here with the smokes." Shyla responded with a smirk on her face.

"Well, I guess you can come on in." Cashmere said, as she opened the screen door to let Dirty in. "Sit down." She said, while giving Shyla the stank face.

"Cash, I didn't know you were still smoking." Shyla mumbled, as Cashmere shot her the side-eye.

"You done stop smoking that fast?" Dirty asked.

"No, Shyla need to hush. I'm getting 'bout tired of her ass."

"Oh, I thought—"

"You ain't thought shit Shyla," Cashmere cut in. "Really?! I'm 'bout 1 second away—"

"Okaaaaay, damn." Shyla butted in.

I can't believe this bitch 'bout to say something about me being pregnant. Like it's anybody's business. It ain't even hers. She thought, as she rolled her eyes at her cousin.

Shyla smacked her lips, and then looked over at Dirty. "You gon' roll that shit or nah?"

"You smoke in here now?" Dirty asked Cashmere.

"Hell no," Cashmere responded. "But you know what? Fuck it, it ain't like Jabari will be bringing his ass over here any time soon."

"Damn, y'all over, over?"

"Yep, it seems that way." Cashmere responded. "I'm just over, over it."

"Damn, I thought y'all would've gotten back together by now."

"Well, as you can see that ain't happened and I ain't worried about it." She responded. "So, but where you been? Yo' ass don't ever stay home no more. Be gone weeks at a time."

Dirty glanced up from rolling the blunt. "I've been out of town with my lady. I'll actually be moving at the end of the week."

Cashmere's eyes widened. "You're moving?"

"Yea, I think it's about that time." Dirty answered.

By: Tiece

"What are you gonna do with your house?" Shyla pondered, as Dirty lit the blunt.

"Hell, I'm keeping it right now, but I may put it on the market in another year or so. I just gotta see how things are going to work with me and my lady. You know how that is. One minute you're good and then the next minute you could be going your separate ways."

"You telling me," Cashmere uttered, as Dirty passed her the blunt. She looked over at Shyla and wasted no time taking a toke of the good stuff, and then she passed it on to her.

Shyla reached for the blunt, instantly hitting it. "Next time we see yo' ass you might be married." She said, as she pulled the blunt again.

"Nah, I ain't ready for that shit." Dirty responded. "You see I ain't even selling my house yet. That's because it's still fresh and when relationships are new it's like the honeymoon stages, but what counts is when that honeymoon phase is over."

"Hopefully, it's never over." Shyla said, as she passed Dirty the blunt.

"If only the world operated like that it would be a better place." Dirty said, as he toked on the blunt a few quick times, holding in the smoke and then releasing it. He then passed the blunt back to Cashmere.

Damn, that rotation was fast, she thought. The days before now, she went through the stages of wanting to smoke to ease her nerves, but now after smoking she was having ill feelings, as thoughts of her baby began to play on her judgment. "I'm good. Here Shy." She said, just as her front door unexpectedly opened.

"Oh, so you still smoking?" Jabari asked, the minute he walked in.

Chapter Three

Cashmere's heart dropped, as Shyla took the blunt out of her hand.

"Oh damn," Shyla whispered.

Dirty cleared his throat while quickly standing to his feet. "Wassup B?" he said, reaching out to shake his hand.

Thoughts of wanting to knock him out crossed Jabari's mind, but quickly he gathered his composure long enough to shake his hand.

"I was leaving. I just came over to give Shyla something to smoke." He said, and without waiting for a response he wasted no time dipping.

"Welp, I guess that's my queue." Shyla mumbled, as she stood up. "Wassup Jabari?" she said.

Jabari didn't say a word.

"Cash I'll call you later."

Oh, now you wanna leave, but when I was trying to kick yo' ass out you wouldn't go. Cashmere thought, but then quickly focused her attention back on Jabari. *What the fuck?!!* She nervously thought.

Shyla walked by Jabari with an edgy smile on her face. She felt it best to not say another word, as she hurriedly made her exit.

Jabari closed the door shut behind Shyla, as he mean-mugged Cashmere. "So, you still smoking?"

"Why? It ain't none your business." She said with an attitude.

"If that baby mine it is my business."

"Nah, you act like it ain't yours, so keep that same energy, my nigga."

Jabari frowned. "My nigga? I'm telling you Cashmere, now ain't the time to be fucking with me."

"I don't know why you tripping. I ain't smoke nothing anyway. I was going to, but I thought about it and was handing it back to Shyla."

"Let me smell your breath."

Cashmere frowned. "You ain't wanna be in my face earlier, so don't come tryna smell my breath now."

"I ain't never hit a woman before, but I swear if you weren't pregnant I'd jack yo' ass up." Jabari told her, as he made it a lil further into the living room.

"And, you'll be sitting yo' ass in jail somewhere."

"Cashmere, you got one mo' time to pop off with that sass." He said, walking over to stand in front of her. He had no intentions of jacking her up, but maybe if she thought he would she'd tame her mouthpiece.

"Get from in front of me." Cashmere responded in a high-pitched tone, as she tried to push him to the side. "Moooove!"

"I ain't moving nowhere."

"What's your problem Jabari? You come over here unannounced like you running something, but didn't have shit to say to me earlier."

"That wasn't the time or the place." He told her.

"And, now you think this is the time and place?"

"Yea, which is why I came over here, but I could smell the weed before I even walked up on the porch. And, your door was cracked, so that's why I just walked in. But, I didn't expect you to be smoking."

"I wasn't smoking," Cashmere responded with a roll of the eyes.

Jabari ignored her. "You in here talking to Dirty? What's up with that? He don't come over here, at least I ain't never known him to be over here."

"You act like Dirty was the only one in here. I don't fuck with Dirty like that. He only came over to give Shyla some weed. It was her brilliant idea in the first place to smoke and she asked him to come in, so I joined 'em."

"So, you say."

"It's the truth," Cashmere said. "Why you in here all in my face, anyway? Go to your new girlfriend. I'm gonna be alright."

"She ain't my girlfriend."

"That ain't what it looks like to me." Cashmere told him.

"Quit looking so hard and maybe you won't see shit that ain't got nothing to do with you."

"Yea, whatever." Cashmere uttered. "What you want me to do, because I ain't got time for this?"

"What you mean by that?" Jabari pondered.

"I'm 6 weeks pregnant and I can have an abortion if you don't want this baby. That's what I mean."

"So, you don't want the baby now?"

Cashmere scowled. "Did you hear me say that? I said, if you don't want the baby I'll have an abortion, because I'm not going back and forth with you no more. I'm not gonna sit here feeling less than because you have doubts. They have DNA tests if you didn't know that, so you could always find out the truth. I'm not lying to you." She said with the most serious expression she could muster up. However, her feelings were hurt that Jabari was doing her wrong and all she wanted was for things to go back to how they used to be.

"Do you want the baby Cash?" Jabari asked, as he sat down on the sofa beside her.

"Yes, I want my baby."

"So, don't give me no options. If you want to have the baby, you have the baby."

"But, I also want my baby to have a loving father in his life."

"If the baby is mine, I'll be in her life 100 percent. You wouldn't have to worry about that. I'll take care of my seed."

"Why you calling it a her?" Cashmere asked.

"Why you calling it a him?" he questioned back. They looked over at each other and laughed out loud. For a minute, they had ceased fire for the sake of the baby. Jabari sat quietly for a moment, as things turned serious. "I'm sorry if I've been distant. I'm just going through some things losing Slick and I still can't come to terms with it. Shit still breaks my heart. It's so unbelievable that he's gone."

"I know. We all feel bad about what happened to Slick, but you don't have to shy away from me. I'm not your enemy and I wasn't trying to trap you by getting pregnant. Hell, I was just as surprised as you were, I promise you that. I wasn't looking to be having a baby this soon. I at least wanted to wait until I was around 30ish. But, when I found out, I was excited; and I texted you to let you know because I was hoping you'd be excited too. Maybe it would be our way of getting past ill feelings, so we could be cordial towards each other because of the baby. I get now that it was bad timing."

"I don't wanna say bad timing. You just told me at a time of learning that my best friend was killed. I couldn't be happy for the baby because I was too sad and mad about Slick."

"Not only that, but you aren't even sure if it's yours. Why do you keep feeling that way?" she pondered. "It's embarrassing as fuck."

Jabari simply looked over at her, not really knowing what to say. She had tears in her eyes, making him feel bad for her. What if the baby was his? He'd feel like shit for treating her unkindly or being disrespectful. A part of him still wondered what it would be like to settle down with her, but another part of him just wasn't feeling it no more. How could he have such unresolved feelings over a situation that was supposed to be over?

"Look, B." She said with a serious stare.

"B huh?" he handsomely grinned. She never called him that.

Cashmere smiled, feeling it was time for them to have this adult conversation. If nothing else, he might see a different side of her. "I don't want things to be awkward between us. I know how you feel about this situation. Saying I was pregnant blindsided us both. You were trying to move on, and truth is I was stuck. I didn't know how to move on, because I was still trying to figure out how I could let us go. I know you think I've cheated at some point in our relationship, and there is nothing I can do to prove to you that I haven't, even if I had. What I'm trying to say is that I'm not perfect, definitely flawed by default, but I would never ever want to hurt you. Those aren't and will never be my intentions. I hope you can understand that and give me another chance someday."

Jabari sat quietly, thinking over every single word that left Cashmere's mouth. What she didn't reiterate was that she hadn't cheated, but maybe she'd said it enough and was trying to rephrase it. He looked over at her. Her eyes were genuine, and her heart was pouring sincere words that he'd never heard. He didn't know if he should shut it down or simply stand in the rain in hopes of possibly giving her another chance again. Quickly, that thought left his mind, as he considered his next words wisely before speaking.

"Cash I would like nothing more than for us to be friends. Cool and cordial without the drama. I can't say that I see us getting back together or not, and no it's not about another woman." He explained. "Tiana is a friend of mine and we have good conversation."

"Is that all? Just good conversation huh?"

"Well," Jabari said, with a hunch of the shoulders. He didn't want to lie, but he didn't want to tell her the truth either. "Anyway," he said as indication to steer the conversation back to what he was trying to say. "I don't want no beef with you; especially if, well—" he caught himself. "With you being pregnant with my seed."

Cashmere smiled, just to hear him say that the baby was his seed made her feel 100 times better. "I want us to get along. But, you gotta understand that I'm living my life right now. That ain't got nothing against you, but I don't want or need you popping up where I'm at. That ain't cool and you can't think it's right. What if you and Tiana would've gotten into a fight? Like you can do that in the shape you're in. The last thing you should be thinking about is fighting."

"I know. It was poor judgement, but I'd gotten so heated I didn't know what to do. You weren't returning my calls, on top of that you weren't fucking with me at all. I was just over here in my feelings, emotional as hell, and pregnant. You know I turn into a gangsta 'bout my nigga." She joked, causing Jabari to grin. "Well, correction, my baby daddy."

"I was wrong for that. I was being selfish and caught up in my feelings. I'm sorry."

"Apology accepted." She said with a pleasant smile. "I'm sorry too for showing up to your family's place of business. I knew better and Shyla warned me the whole ride out there."

"Well, that's in the past now." He told her. "Maybe this is what I needed to help me get through this phase of my life. You know all of this is unbelievable. I lost a brother, but a new life is already brewing." He explained with a saddened look on his face while getting choked up. "Damn, I miss him."

I do too, Cashmere thought. She was deeply saddened by Slick's death, but she could only show those emotions while she was alone. She couldn't even let Shyla see her crying over Slick. It was nobody's business how much that affected her. "You okay?" she asked as she looked over at Jabari.

He was looking like he'd been going through it. His eyes were watery and red. He had bags that looked like he hadn't gotten any rest in weeks. "Nah, I ain't okay. I ain't gon' even lie. I'm sick, straight sick."

"Are you at least eating?"

"I don't have much of an appetite."

"Yea, but did you put something on your stomach today?" she worriedly asked.

Jabari shook his head. "No," he answered.

Cashmere stood up from the sofa. "I'll cook you a steak, because you need something to eat."

"Nah, you ain't gotta do that."

"Yes, I do. I need my child's father alive and well; not pushing up daisy's because his ass wouldn't eat." She joked, getting a smile to appear on his face.

"Once I'm finished cooking, you can eat and then you can leave." She told him. She didn't want him to think she was trying to get him to stay. Maybe if she treated him like it was nothing between them besides the baby, that he'd finally come around.

"Damn, you gon' just put me out like that?"

"Hell yea!" Cashmere teased with a hearty laugh. She really wanted to pick his brain about Tiana, but she figured that now wasn't the time. Maybe he'd open up sooner than later. She just hated being on the outside looking in. She headed into the kitchen, while still talking to Jabari. "When are you gonna invite me to your crib?"

"I don't know. For one, yo' ass don't know how to act. I might have company."

Cashmere peeked her head back in the living room. "OH, so now you admit that you're talking to her?"

"No, I'm not admitting nothing. Me and her aren't together. We're just cool friends."

By: Tiece

"Cool friends with benefits?" Cashmere pondered.

"We're just cool, that's all you need to know."

"You're fucking her."

"Whatever Cashmere." Jabari said with a shake of the head.

Cashmere grinned with a shake of the head. Things were awkward as is when talking about him being with another woman, but she had to deal with it some kind of way. Why not joke about it, at least that would help ease the pain. She cooked Jabari's steak and by the time she returned with his plate, he was sleep.

"Jabari, you gon' eat?" she asked him, with a slight shake on his shoulder.

He moved a little while cracking his eyes. "Just sit it right there." He told her, and with that he rested his head back on the sofa, eyes back shut.

Cashmere sat the plate down on the large ottoman in front of him. "Well, guess that's my queue to take a shower." She uttered. "Your food is in front of you." She called out in a loud tone, as she headed down the hallway. She didn't know if he'd wake up, eat his steak and then leave or if he'd join her in the bedroom for the rest of the night. However, what she did know was that for once she was putting her feelings first and if he stayed he stayed. If he didn't, he didn't. Either way, she was just good with knowing they were back on good terms. That meant that anything was possible. All she had to do was play her cards right to keep it that way.

Chapter Four

The next morning Cashmere woke up feeling sick, not just throwing up but thinking about the good men she'd lost. She had not only lost Jabari, she lost Slick too. Even though their affair would've been scowled upon, she still had feelings for him. They had gotten quite close right before his passing, so to get the phone call that he'd been killed was devasting. She had cried about it every day since it happened.

After vomiting her guts up, she decided that she'd get out the house for some fresh air. She couldn't take laying around for another day. Thoughts of messaging Jabari crossed her mind, but then she decided against it. Instead, she grabbed her purse and headed out to her car. A drive over to Shyla's house was much needed, as she started the ignition, turned up her music and then headed in that direction.

Within fifteen minutes, she was pulling up in Shyla's driveway to park, and then turned off the ignition. It didn't look like nobody was home, but then again Shyla liked parking in her two-car garage. Cashmere shook her head. Somehow, Shyla had lucked-up and struck it rich by fucking with a nigga that belonged to somebody else. What kind of bad, good luck was that? She sat parked for a minute, drying her eyes. Sometimes, the tears were never-ending. She got out the car, and then proceeded to the front door. She rang the doorbell a couple of times, and then Shyla opened the door.

"What you want? You come here to apologize?" she pondered.

Cashmere sadly looked at her. "I'm sorry. I know I acted an ass yesterday and I was too deep in my feelings, but I shouldn't have taken it out on you."

"Awwww Bestie," Shyla smiled, as she reached out to give her a hug. "I'm sorry too. I didn't mean to be so hard on you. I know you've been going through it."

"Thank you," Cashmere softly responded.

"Come on," Shyla told her, as Cashmere followed her to the kitchen area.

Cashmere sat down on one of the bar stools in front of the oval black and white granite countertop surrounding the island stove. "It smells good in here. Looks like I came just in time."

"You know I'll feed you in a heartbeat; especially now," she joked.

"I knoooow," Cashmere chuckled. "Where is Ryder and River?"

"With yo' auntie. She should be stopping by soon to drop them off. She kept 'em last night."

"Oh okay. It's a blessing to have auntie in your life. She steps up and helps you with the boys all the time. She's always been that way."

"Yea, but mom isn't perfect."

"Neither is mine, but for them to be sisters you'd think mine would've learned a lesson or two from yours."

"Mom did say that she's been trying to change her life." Shyla told her.

"I highly doubt that. Everything is always about her. Her drinking, her men, her lifestyle, her drugs—" she paused, then continued. "That she think nobody knows she's using."

"Girl hush," Shyla grinned. "She do keep up the habit better than other people that are pill popping. Your mama still looks good, too. She thinks she still twenty-years old and in college. She stays high off life—"

"Correction, PILLS, preferably Ecstasy or Adderall if she can't get the X pill."

Shyla laughed under her breath. "Leave my auntie alone. If that's what makes her forget what that nigga did to y'all then let her be. At least he ain't making a fool out of her no more."

"That's because she's making a fool out of herself." Cashmere slid in.

"I think she's in a better headspace. I know that might sound funny, but it's true. I think," she said. "She's just living now and fucking all the fine ass college boys."

"Ewwwww, watch yo' mouth bitch." Cashmere joked, causing Shyla to bust out laughing.

"I'm just saying." Shyla teased. "She keeps her a fine ass youngan around."

"Them boys be younger than us."

"But they're older than eighteen and that's all that matters. Let that woman deal with life how she sees fit now. I used to be mad at her, but I've come to realize that she's trying. She may not be perfect, but she was able to get over Earl."

"Look at God," Cashmere uttered.

"You should be glad about that. Y'all damn near went to war 'bout Earl. I don't who was crazier. At one point he had both of y'all defending his actions and bickering back and forth with each other. I'm just glad that finally you woke up and moved in with us. However, auntie still stayed with that nigga. He basically treated her like shit after that."

"And she put up with that dumb shit for a few more years after I'd left. He still would've been there if it weren't for her walking in and catching him in her bed with another bitch." Cashmere said, while thinking back.

"That's why I said to let auntie live. Hell, she done been through enough over the years."

"I guess." Cashmere said, just as Rich entered the kitchen. *Oh damn*, she thought, then spoke. "Hey Rich."

"Wassup Cashmere." He responded, while walking over by the stove and giving Shyla a kiss.

"You leaving so soon? I thought you were staying a few days." She asked while noticing that he was carrying his Louis Vuitton backpack in his hand.

"Yea, I was planning on staying a few days, but I gotta get back. It's something going on with the new club and it needs my attention." He told her.

"Okay," Shyla said with a disappointed expression. "I was just cooking breakfast."

"I'm sorry babe. Give Cashmere my part." He told her, as he kissed her once more and then headed for the front door.

"Damn, he be doing it like that?" Do he ever stay long?"

Shyla smacked her lips. "Hell, he barely comes and when he does it's just like now. He comes for a night or two and then he's gone."

"How do you feel about that?"

Shyla shrugged her shoulders while stirring the grits. "I don't know. I thought it was gonna be better than before. His wife and kids are on the West Coast which meant that our time together should've gotten better when he visited. I thought he was going to really step up to be a father to his kids, but that hasn't happened much either. Honestly, I'm tired of playing second fiddle. On top of that, running the clubs are becoming a hassle. I keep getting into it with the girls because they're jealous about me and Rich's relationship. They don't feel like that position should've gone to me. But, hell I got two kids by him they should know better."

"But they don't because nobody knows he has kids by you, but a select few."

"But still, and it ain't their business, anyway."

"I feel you," Cashmere responded.

"It just seems like something isn't right with Rich. I don't know what, but I feel like I'll find out soon enough."

"What's done in the dark will come to the light."

Shyla nodded her head. "You got that right." She agreed. "But girl, I'm talking about Justin."

Cashmere smirked giving her cousin the side-eye. "What about Justin?"

"That nigga smelled so good when he grabbed me yesterday. I didn't realize he'd gotten that fine. I was like, daaaaammmnn. Maybe it was a good thing we went out there. Well, a good thing for me, but not for you."

"Girl stop it. I can't believe you're actually interested in somebody other than Rich."

"I told you, I'm tired of Rich. Who don't want to settle down with somebody someday? I can't do that with Rich and from the looks of things, he ain't planning on leaving his wife no time soon."

"Thought I'd never hear you say that." Cashmere mumbled.

"Hush," Shyla uttered back. "You want me to fix you something to eat? Some grits?"

"Yea fix me some grits. Put a lil cheese in 'em." Cashmere requested. "This baby have me so damn sick I don't know what to do. I'm tired of throwing up and shit."

"Hopefully, you should be able to hold the grits down. They do stick to you." Shyla explained. "So, what happened after me and Dirty left last night? Did Jabari stay?"

"He stayed, but I don't even know when he left. We had words for a little while, but then we got over it. I'm trying to show him a different side of me. I just hope that we can work on being cordial parents. He still denies that bitch, but I know better. They might be friends, but they're fucking each other. I can bet you that."

Shyla nodded her head, as she sat the bowl of hot grits in front of Cashmere. "I can believe you." She agreed.

"He was definitely pissed about Dirty being in the house and us smoking."

"Nah, bitch he was pissed that you was smoking. So, does that mean that he's claiming the baby now?"

"Yea, I guess. He act like he's going to stop giving me a hard time."

"Well, I'm always rooting for y'all. You've slowed down a lot, so I hope that counts for something too."

"I hope so too." Cashmere told her. As she sat there eating her grits her cell phone chirped of an incoming text message.

Hey ma, thanks for the steak last night. It was good. JAH

You're welcome. CASHMERE

I may come over later if I'm not too busy. I gotta get ready for this rematch against Roy. He think he did something being that he beat Bruno the last time. JAH

Okay, that'll be cool. I'm just chilling with Shyla right now, but if you come later I'll be back home by then. CASHMERE

Okay, good. Are you good? Hru feeling? JAH

I'm feeling good. Woke up sick this morning, but overall, I'm good. Shyla cooked grits, so now I'm trying to replenish my system. Lol CASHMERE

The baby have yo' ass sick, huh? JAH

Every day, but I have an appointment in two weeks. I'll be 2 months then. If you wanna go you're welcome to. CASHMERE

Yea, I would like that. JAH

Okay good. Well, I don't wanna hold you up but I appreciate you texting. Means more than you know. CASHMERE

Fa sho'. JAH

Cashmere smiled while sitting her phone down next to her bowl.

"That must've been Jabari texting you. That's the only time I see a smile like that on your face."

"Yep, that was him. I'm just trying to stay in my lane and not do too much. I don't wanna push him away and I don't want things to be no more awkward for us than they already are."

"Wow, that's growth Bestie. That's growth." Shyla encouraged with an approving smile back.

"Coming in," Net said, as she entered the house with River and Ryder.

"We're in the kitchen Mama." Shyla called out.

The boys ran into the kitchen and immediately ran over to Shyla for a hug. They were very handsome little boys and was quite smart for their ages. "Hey Mommy," they spoke almost in unison.

"Hey sons." She spoke back, giving each one a kiss on the lips.

Cashmere smiled at how close their bond was. She couldn't wait to share the same thing with her baby.

"Hey Cash," they spoke, as she called them over to hug on 'em for a second.

"I've missed y'all. Y'all are never home or with your mother."

"Yea, because they're always with me." Net said, as she entered the kitchen. "Hey Cash."

"Hey Auntie."

"It's been a while since I saw you last. You don't ever come to visit me no more."

"Auntie don't take it personal. You know I love you. I just have a lot going on."

"Well, you shouldn't take so long to visit the people that love you. Life is short and anything can happen at any given time. Love those that love you."

"I know Auntie. You're right and I apologize. I'll come visit more." She told her.

"Mommy where is daddy?" River asked. He was the 3-year-old going on 25.

"He left baby." She responded.

"He's gone so soon?" Net nosily pondered with a frown on her face. "I think him moving to the West Coast was actually a bad move for you. He spent more time with the boys when he lived on this end."

"I know right," Shyla uttered.

"I know you can't possibly think that this is going to change. He's not the man you want him to be. I can't tell you that enough. The only good thing you got out of this was those two beautiful boys. I never cared for him. You know that. I just don't feel like he has your best interest at heart, let alone River and Ryder. I don't regret my babies I just wish you had them by somebody else."

"You wasn't talking like that when he gave you a thousand dollars and said you didn't have to pay it back."

"Of course, I was nice then. I needed to get my damn plumbing fixed. Shit was backing up in every damn drain in the house." She responded, without a care in the world. "I couldn't even shower without shit coming through the drain."

"Ewwwww auntie."

Net shrugged her shoulders. "I'm just saying and Rich ain't no good. Not for you, not for the boys and not for his wife. He can tell that lie to somebody else. Hell, he might have another whole family on the West Coast. Who knows why he just packed his family up and moved?"

"He opened another club there. He knows where business is booming at. Plus, her family lives there."

"His don't." Net said.

"Mama you do the most." Shyla uttered. "I don't like when you talk like that around them."

"You better start teaching your boys the real. Don't have them growing up with white people issues just because you're trying to protect their father. It is what it is." Net bluntly explained, and just that quickly, she focused her attention back on Cashmere. "When was the last time you talked to your mama?"

"Even longer than the last time I talked to you." Cashmere responded. "You know our relationship ain't all that. I love her, but I just choose to love her from afar."

"You shouldn't treat her like that. At the end of the day, she is your mother." Net told her. "Sometimes, you have to forgive and let go."

"I agree, but Mama still have a lot going on. She's dating more and is a bit of a wild child now. I probably act older than her."

"She's just living her life. I know she's not perfect, but she's coming around. She even mentioned to me the other day that she missed having you around."

"Oh really?" Cashmere pondered.

"Yes, really and you should go see her; especially because of that." Net explained.

Cashmere shrugged her shoulders. "I don't know. I'll think about it."

"Think harder about the baby inside of you." Net said, as Cashmere shot Shyla the side-eye.

Talking ass bitch, she thought.

"Don't deny your mama the right to meet her grandbaby. They have a way of changing a person for the better. I mean, look at mine. I love being around them and wouldn't trade 'em for the world."

"I guess," Cashmere uttered.

"I think you and auntie need to go to counseling together. That may be a way for y'all to reconcile and get over the past. Not only will that be good for you, but auntie can definitely benefit from it too." Shyla encouraged, as she fixed the boys some breakfast. "Mama, you hungry?"

"No, I got other plans this morning, so I'll talk to y'all later." Net said, as she kissed Shyla on the cheek, and then Cashmere on hers. She then hugged the boys. "Grandma loves you. Call me later if y'all mama get tired of you." She joked.

Shyla laughed out loud. "Quit playing Mama."

"Your mama is a got-damn trip." Cashmere laughed.

"She ain't gon' never change." Shyla grinned.

"Well, what you think?"

Shyla frowned. "Think about what?" she asked, while sitting the boy's food in front of them on the table.

"What your mom said? What are you gonna do about that situation?"

Shyla hunched her shoulders. "I don't know, but what I do know is that I'm gonna have to sit down and have a long talk with him. He needs to know that I'm not waiting around and that eventually, I'm gonna talk to somebody else."

"Mommy, you're gonna get us a new daddy?" River asked.

Shyla looked over at Cashmere with a shocked expression, and then answered her son. "No, River. You'll always have the same daddy. Mommy is just gonna get a new friend, a guy friend. Not right now, but one day." She told him. Maybe it was time for her to start keeping it real just like her mama had said, and what better time to start than now.

Chapter Five

Jabari drove by the street that Slick lived on. He could barely even look in that direction. Thoughts of how much fun they'd had while chilling at his house, playing ball, talking shit, and enjoying life sat heavily on his heart. He missed his brother to no ends and just wished he could have him back. He looked over at Cain over in the passenger seat. He seemed to be having the same thoughts as sadness covered his face.

"You a'ight Bruh?" Jabari asked.

"Yea, I'm good. I just still can't believe it." Cain responded with a shake of the head.

"Me, either. I haven't even had the guts to in there yet. His mama told me that I'm welcome to go in and get anything I needed or wanted out of it, but it's just too painful right now."

"I feel you, Bruh. The shit is still fresh, but if you need me to go with you just let me know. I'll be there for you."

"I appreciate that Bruh." Jabari responded. "So, how do you feel about going over here to see Cannon?"

Cain shrugged his shoulders. "I'm happy to see my lil man, but I would've preferred to do it at my house. It's just easier that way. You know why I asked you to come, right?"

"Yea, because you figured Lauren will be more at ease if she knows you're being chaperoned." He grinned.

"You know me pretty well," Cain laughed. "I know if I go over here by myself not only will Lauren feel some type of way, but this hood girl might try to rape me." He joked but was dead ass.

Jabari laughed. "I don't know how you managed to fuck her with no condom."

"Hell, me either. The only thing I can blame it on is the alcohol." He grinned. "But, no, seriously. Shawty is pretty as hell. She got a tight lil body and she got good pussy, but she don't think like us. She ain't but 22 years old and is hooder than a muthafucka. I wouldn't have ever thought she'd even want a baby; not how wild she is. Why you think I had to have a paternity test?"

"I feel ya, Bruh. I would've had to have one too. You can't be too careful these days."

"I wanted to stop by and see my daughter too, but her mama ain't even responded to my text yet."

"She mad or something?"

"Nah, me and Hazel ain't really had no major issues. She just has separation anxiety. Meaning, my daughter ain't used to staying with nobody, but her. So, I'm cool with that, but now I've realized that I need to step up more. Start being a presence in her life. Hazel don't have a problem with it, but she's a little like Sofia. Nevaeh can't come to my house, because Lauren is there."

"Craaazy." Jabari uttered. "But, that's because you don't go around her like that. You gotta do better with that Bruh. If the mamas see how you are with their babies, they'll know that you wouldn't let nobody hurt 'em, harm 'em, or mistreat 'em. If they can't see that relationship, then their gonna always have problems with you keeping the babies overnight."

"I know," Cain responded. "Tryna keep down chaos with Lauren; especially when it comes to Hazel."

"Why you say that?"

"Because Hazel got business about herself. She's sophisticated and bougie with it. She fine as hell too. I ain't gon' lie. I like shawty a lot, but I love Lauren more, so I just stay away to keep down the peace. I send her money and shit, though."

"That ain't the same though Bruh."

"I know." Cain said with a nod of the head. "I'm gon' do better. I ain't got no choice and that's what I told Lauren. She gotta accept my kids or maybe it ain't meant for us to be together."

"She'll accept 'em because y'all are meant to be together. Both of y'all asses crazy as hell."

Cain laughed, as they pulled into The Gardens, low-income based apartments that sat directly in the heart of the worst part of the city.

"Damn, I'm surprised they ain't knocked these shits down yet." Jabari uttered.

"I know, right and just to imagine my boy lives over here." He said, with a shake of the head.

Jabari drove into the neighborhood, on each side of him were worn down apartment buildings. Kids were running up and down the sidewalk, as others sat on their porches being nosey.

"Right here Bruh." Cain said, as Jabari turned in an empty parking spot and parked. "Don't just sit there. You going in here with me."

"Maaaaannn," Jabari groaned.

"Come on." Cain insisted.

"I know you wanna spend time with your son, but can't I just drop you off and then come back and get you?"

Cain frowned. "Hell nawl." He said with a serious face.

Jabari bust out laughing. "Nigga, I'm just messing with you. You know I'm going in here. I don't want to, but I will."

"Boy, I was about to say," Cain grinned, as they got out of the car.

"Ayyyye, wassup?" a boy said as he walked up on Jabari. "It's the Goat y'all." He said to his lil homeboys.

Jabari smiled. "Wassup lil man?"

"We watched your last race on YouTube." He said with a big smile on his face like Jabari was a celebrity.

"It was a good race too," another boy said, as he ran up to join the conversation.

"Man, ol' Roy didn't stand a chance." The first boy laughed.

"You right Bruh." The second boy agreed, as they gave each other high-five. Then out of nowhere, he blurted out. "His mama got a crush on you."

Jabari and Cain laughed out loud.

"What you know about a crush?" Jabari teased. "How old are you?"

"I'm 13, but am I lying Bruh?" he asked his homey, while anxiously showing all his teeth.

The first boy nodded his head to agree. "She do have a crush on you." He admitted.

"Well, tell her I said wassup, when you see her."

"I will." He excitedly responded. "Aye, can me and my homeys take a picture with you?"

Jabari nodded his head. "Yea," he answered.

"Aye, you'll take this picture for me?" the first boy asked Cain.

"Yea, y'all stand next to him." Cain beamed inside, as three other boys walked over and kneeled down in front of the Jabari. The other two stood on each side of him. Cain always loved moments like this. It kept Jabari grounded. It also reminded him that people looked up to him, whether that was to win races or to be a mentor. Cain took about 3 pictures and then handed the boy his cell phone back.

"Thanks, Bruh," he said with a big smile. "I'm 'bout to put this on IG."

"Tag me in it." One of the boys said.

"Me too, Bruh," another one said.

"Shit, I'm 'bout to run in the house and tell mama I just saw The Goat." The first boy chimed in before he took off running.

Jabari and Cain laughed as they walked off. Jabari looked back. "Y'all hold it down and stay in school. Ain't nothing out here in these streets."

"Yes sir," they nearly responded in unison.

Just as they walked up to the front door, it flew open. Sofia stood in the doorway with a very short blue jean skirt on, a fitted lavender tank top, and a lavender pair of flip flops. She had butt-length microbraids that were rainbow colored with the acrylic, sharp pointed nails to match.

"Wassup, baby daddy or shall I say, sperm donor." She joked with a serious expression. "Y'all come in. Wassup up, B?"

"Wassup Sofia." He spoke back.

"Y'all sit down. I'll go get Cannon. He's in the back with my sister. She just washed and dressed him." She explained, and then disappeared down the hall.

"Damn, it's trash all over the place." Jabari said, as he looked around. The minute he sat on the loveseat, the right end of it hit the floor causing him to jump back up.

"What the fuck?!" Cain exclaimed, as he looked under the loveseat. The legs were gone. "Damn, it's sitting on 2 bricks." He then picked the end of the sofa up and sat it back down on top of the 2 bricks.

"I'll just sit over here Bruh." Jabari said with a slight grin under his breath. Instead, he sat at the dining room table. The chairs there looked pretty sturdy.

Sofia returned with Cannon in her arms. Cain looked him over, as he reached for him. Cannon was dressed in a cute Nike romper with a pair of Jordan's on his feet. He smelled good and his face was clean. *Why you ain't having him looking like this when you brought him over?* He thought. "Hey daddy's man." He said, while kissing his baby.

"This your first time seeing him B?" Sofia asked, as she looked at Jabari.

"Yea, it's my first time seeing him in person." He answered, being that Cain had already showed him pictures that she'd been posting all over social media.

"Don't he look just like his daddy?"

"Yea, he does," Jabari responded, as he looked over at his nephew. "He's gonna be a lil heartbreaker."

"Why you ain't clean up this place?" Cain intervened with a frown. "My boy can't be crawling on this junky ass floor. You want him to put the wrong thing in his mouth and swallow it?"

"Now, you wanna play father of the year, huh?"

"Nah, I'm just a father that's concerned about the well-being of my son."

Sofia smacked her lips and rolled her eyes. "Yea whatever." She uttered.

"I'm serious. You need to clean this shit up." He said in a firmer tone.

"Okaaay, damn." Sofia said, as she got up and started to clean up the front area of the house.

Cain sat on the sofa playing with Cannon, as Jabari's thoughts reflected to Cashmere being pregnant. Just catching her with a blunt in her hand pissed him off. So, he knew he couldn't deal with no baby mama like Sofia. Thoughts of Tiana crossed his mind. He had yet to say anything about the incident that had occurred the day before. A part of him knew he had to reach out at some point, but maybe not just yet. He had to think about what he'd say and prepare himself for what she might respond in return.

"Aye Bruh, let me hold him." Jabari chimed in, as Cain stood up and passed him Cannon.

"Wassup nephew." Jabari smiled, as he bounced him up and down on his lap. "He don't miss a bottle, that's for sure." He added, feeling how solid the little one was with his juicy thighs and jiggly jaws. It wasn't bad at all playing with the little one.

"Nah, he's real greedy." Sofia laughed. "Aye, come here. Let me holla at you real quick."

Cain looked over at her. "What you mean?"

"I mean, follow me to my bedroom. I can't have a private talk with you right quick? I ain't tryna rape you."

Jabari laughed out loud. "You heard her Bruh. She ain't tryna rape you."

Cain grinned with a shake of the head. "She better not," he clowned while getting up and following Sofia down the hall. "Hold it down Bruh. I'll be right back." He assured him.

Jabari nodded his head, while he continued to play with the baby.

"Wassup Sofia?" Cain asked the minute they stepped into her bedroom.

She closed the door shut behind them.

"You ain't gotta do all that," he told her.

"Chill out." She aggressively told him. "Sit down."

Cain looked around. The bedroom wasn't as junky as the front area, but he didn't want to sit on a bed that 100 other niggas had sat on. "Nah, I'm good."

"I don't know why you're acting like this. I just want you to be a good father to our son."

"You should let me take him home with me then."

Sofia frowned. "Today?" she pondered.

"Yea," he nodded. "Why not?"

"For one, I don't like your bitch—"

"She ain't no bitch. I don't let her disrespect you and I'm not gon' let you disrespect her."

"Oh, she be talking about me?"

"Not at all, but it was some things said that day y'all got into it. Nevertheless, I said what I said."

"Okay," Sofia nodded. A part of her felt good to know that if anything was said about her that he straightened it.

Cain stood there just trying to say anything, so she'd allow him to take the baby back to his house. The last thing he wanted to do was sit at her house for a longer period of time than he planned to, son or no son. Even when they'd fuck, he was always in and out like a thief in the night.

"So, what are your plans? I don't wanna take out child support, but—"

"But nothing. I'll make sure he's straight and I'll give you money when you need it."

"It sounds good." She uttered, giving him the side-eye.

"Don't play with me. You know since I found out he was mine I've been making sure he's straight. I bet you bought him that outfit he has on with the money I gave you."

Sofia nodded her head. "You're right. I got a him a few outfits and some J's, so he can be like his daddy. I also got him a gray pair of Huaraches."

Cain smiled. "I like that." He told her. "Make sure you always keep my boy fresh. You should never bring him out the house unless he's straight. He's one of us now."

"What you gon' do about his last name, since he's one of y'all now?"

"I'm gon' get his name changed to McCoy. You ain't gotta worry. We can do that this week."

"Okay sounds good to me. I can meet you at the place. Just let me know when."

"I will," Cain responded. "Now is there anything else we need to talk about?"

"You should let me give you some head. I always loved sucking on that big dick." She smirked.

"Girl, you know I ain't here for that."

"You should be," she said while sticking her hand under her skirt. She slid her middle finger inside of her thirst-pot and then pulled it out. She seductively looked at him and then sucked on her finger.

Cain's eyes widened, as he fought the urge of an erection.

"Don't you wanna taste it?" she asked with a lick of the lips.

"Nawl, nah, shit I gotta get out of here." He said, trying to push her out the way.

"You shouldn't act like that. Let me give you some head. I promise I won't tell nobody. You should wanna have some sort of sexual relationship with your baby mama."

"You do realize I have 2 of those, right?"

"I ain't thinking about that other bitch. I'm talking about me." She explained, causing Cain to laugh a little.

"I've missed you and if you give me another chance I promise to do right and be good. I might even let Cannon come over for a night."

Cain's curious eyes stretched a bit. "Stop playing."

"I'm serious. All I wanna do is suck your dick. Wassup?"

"Damn, chill out with yo' aggressive ass." He said, as she attempted to unbuckle his belt. "Calm down. You know I can't do this."

"You can do whatever you want to do. I just think we'll have a much better relationship if you let me have my way sometimes."

"Hell nawl," Cain let out after thinking about it carefully. "The first argument we have you'll go running yo' mouth to my lady."

"I ain't stun yo' lady. She ain't got nothing on me. My son is your son. I'm gon' always be around." She told him with a serious stare.

"You say that now." He told her.

"I'm gon' always say that, as long as you play by the rules."

"Hell, I didn't know there were any rules. Guess you learn something new every day."

"I guess so," she mocked. "So, you gon' let me or nah?"

"You gon' let me take my son home today or nah?"

"I'll think about it," she said.

Jabari was still upfront watching busy body get into everything. He had to keep a close eye on him to make sure he didn't put nothing in his mouth. His curly hair and curious bright eyes reminded him so much of Skylar. It was funny how much Cain's son looked just like him, which meant that he also looked like he could've been

Skylar's son, too. People would say that Cain and Skylar looked more alike. It was also said that he and Justin favored more.

"Hey buuuddyy," a lady said, as she came down the hallway. She stopped to give Cannon a kiss on the jaw, and then looked over at Jabari.

"Hey, I'm Yolanda, Sofia's older sister."

"Wassup, I'm Jabari, Cain's brother." He said back.

She walked into the kitchen and opened the refrigerator. "You want something to drink. My sister has some beer and wine coolers in here or you can get some Kool-aide."

Jabari shook his head. "Nah, I'm good." He told her.

She grabbed a watermelon Smirnoff wine cooler and popped the top. She eyed Jabari as he did the same to her.

"You live here too?" he pondered.

"No, I live across town. I just come over to visit my nephew from time to time. Or, I take him with me." She responded.

"Oh okay," he said, but for some reason was glad to hear that she didn't live there too. He sat back admiring the way she played around with Cannon. Kissing on his neck and making him laugh out loud. She was real cute and literally like night and day compared to how Sofia carried herself. She was wearing a short romper that hugged her small curves, showing off a sexy tattoo on her thigh. Tattoos also were seen on other body parts, like her arm, and upper back. An African Woman with a beautiful face and colored lipstick and earrings stood out against her pale, light skin. To him, she favored Kat Tat from Black Ink, cute with a lot of sex appeal and a fatter butt.

"Well, since my sister is locked up in the room with your brother and I don't wanna disturb them, can you tell her that I left? Let her know that I'll come back and get Cannon if she wanted to get out later tonight."

"I'll let her know," Jabari told her.

"It was good to meet you. Maybe I'll see you around." She smiled.

"Yea, maybe." He said back.

She kissed Cannon once more, and then left. Once he'd gotten her sexy ass out of his head, his thoughts moved on to Tiana. For some reason, he couldn't shake her. He pulled out his cell phone and decided to send her a text message, but then decided against it. But before he could think about talking himself out of it again, his phone rang. He glanced down at the display screen.

"Wassup Unc?" he answered.

"Hey Nephew. Where you at? What time you coming out here?"

By: Tiece

"I'm over here to Sofia's house with Cain. He's visiting his son for a little while."

"Oh, I still haven't seen the lil fella yet."

"I'm sure you will, soon enough. Anyway, I don't know what time I'm coming. I know we gotta do a few tests runs, but I'll get 'em in. The race is Sunday. It's only Wednesday."

"I know nephew, but yo' Pops and Bruno have been working on it. They swapped the cam out and added more HP. We need to see how it runs before you race on Sunday. This could be the difference between winning and losing."

"Losing ain't an option, so I feel you. I'll get there by this evening. I guess I'll head out that way after I drop Cain off. He'll probably ride with me though."

"Okay, do that." Papers said. "Aye, you a'ight?"

"Yea, I'm better Unc. You know how it is. I have my days." He answered.

"We all do," Papers said. "Well, if you need me don't hesitate to call."

"I won't." Jabari said, just as Cain showed back up. "A'ight Unc. I'll holla at you later."

"A'ight nephew." Papers said.

Cain picked up Cannon. "You wanna go home with Daddy?"

"Oh, you taking him with you?" Jabari asked, just as he noticed Cain carrying the baby bag on his shoulder.

"Yea," Cain responded.

Sofia returned, with a satisfied look on her face. "If my baby starts crying and won't sleep bring him back home. Oh, and grab his car seat out the backseat of my car."

Cain glanced back at her. "I will."

The minute they were outside and walking to the car, Jabari looked over at his brother with a half-smile on his face. "What'd you do to pull this one off Bruh?"

Chapter Six

Tiana sipped from her glass of wine, as she and Lauren parlayed at her house, watching a little TV. Not only was Jabari on her mind, but Rihanna was a close second. Both had her confused and somewhat in her feelings, and on top of that neither was talking to her.

"Sis, I'm feeling this damn wine already and it's good." Lauren said, as she looked over at Tiana.

"I told you it was good. I get lit off it all the time." Tiana grinned, as she sipped from her glass again.

"I can't find shit for us to watch."

"Click on the firestick and find something there. I heard the new Shaft isn't a bootleg copy. We need to watch something funny to clear our head."

"I agree." Lauren said, as she clicked on the firestick application to watch Shaft through an Exodus download. She found Shaft, but before playing it she got up. "I need to use the bathroom."

Tiana laughed. "Wine will do it to you every time."

"Especially me, my kidneys flush every ten minutes." She joked, and then headed to use the bathroom.

Tiana took in a deep breath and then let it out. She sighed with thoughts of wanting to at least reach out to Rihanna, since she really didn't know what to say to Jabari. She picked up her phone and without second guessing if she should or not, she sent her a message.

How come you've been so distant lately? TIANA

Within seconds, she responded.

Besides Kory being around, I've been more focused on what I have going on. RIHANNA

Oh, so it's like that? & Even if you had been coming around you would know that Kory hasn't. I told you when I put him out he hadn't been welcome back since. TIANA

You always say that until he comes back. RIHANNA

You can save the bullshit for somebody that don't know you. It's more to the story, so what's up? TIANA

Anywayssss, my girl has been acting weird about us hanging out together. RIHANNA

Why? (confused emoji) TIANA

She don't trust us together. She says that even best friends aren't as close as we are. So, I've been laying low. I don't want no smoke. I told you I really like her. RIHANNA

You don't even know her like that. She's already trying to run any relationship outside of the one you have with her. Is she that insecure? TIANA

You would say that because the relationship she's running is the one I have with you. RIHANNA

So, I guess us being besties since before Jesus was born don't count? You & your bitch are tripping. TIANA

By: Tiece

She should have a right to feel that way, though. It ain't like we're JUST BESTIES. We play around from time to time. RIHANNA

Cut the bullshit Rih. We play around maybe twice, no more than three times a year, if that. We're not in high school no more. We both have our own lives and vowed that any extra-curricular activities we indulged in was just that. Nothing more or less which is why we don't do it often. Hell, for about 7 years straight, we didn't do it at all. So, I don't see what the biggie is. At the end of the day you're still my best friend and she's trying to come between that. TIANA

T we'll discuss this later. I gotta go. RIHANNA

Tiana looked up from her phone with an annoyed expression. She shook her head, as she looked over Lauren.

"What's wrong with you? That must've been Jabari you were so caught up messaging."

"Nope."

"Oh God, don't tell me it was Kory with his aggravating ass."

"Nope," Tiana responded again.

"Well, who the hell got you all in your feelings besides them?"

"Rih," Tiana answered.

"Rihanna still acting distant?"

"Yep and she says it's because of her new girlfriend. She doesn't want us hanging out together. She thinks we're closer than we should be as best friends."

"Well, does she know that y'all have been tight since before Jesus was a baby?"

Tiana grinned. "Same thing I told her," she responded. "It's cool though. I'm just not used to us not talking every day."

"She'll come around. If nothing else, I know she loves yo' ass to death." Lauren said. "I always wanted me a best friend like her, but hell, I can't get along with women." She grinned.

"That sounds about right," Tiana laughed. "So, what's going on with you? I missed the baby. I wanted to see him."

"I know, but Cain took him out to the shop to meet Biggs and Papers. Jah has a few test runs and Cain was excited to have his son be a part of that." Lauren explained.

"How do you feel? I mean, how are you feeling about that?"

Lauren shrugged her shoulders, as she poured herself another glass of wine. "I don't know. I was surprised when he walked in with him. He didn't tell me that he was bringing the baby back home. Honestly, I don't even know how him and that crazy gul came to agree on that, being that she must hate my guts."

"Didn't you say she was young? Plus, he talks about her being a wild one—"

"Which is why I can't understand him fucking her, let alone without a condom." Lauren cut in.

"Shit happens." Tiana uttered. "So, back to what I was saying. Maybe she just needs a break."

"Yea, I hope that's all it was." Lauren uttered.

"You gotta learn to trust your man; especially at a time like this. Look at it this way, he was able to bring the baby here instead of having to sit over there with him. So, that must count for something, right?"

"I guess," Lauren answered. "Honestly, I just wasn't prepared this time. The last time I had gotten myself ready to see him. And don't get me wrong, he's the cutest little human ever, but my heart still breaks that he's not mine."

"I understand Sis." Tiana said, as she felt bad for her. "So, what all do you know about his other baby mama? Do he talk about her?"

Lauren shrugged. "I showed you a picture of her on IG before, but that was a at least a year ago. Nevertheless, ain't much changed."

"Her name is Hazel, right?" Tiana asked, as she picked up her phone to look through her IG search engine.

"Yea, Hazel Brown." Lauren nodded.

Tiana pulled her page and scanned through it. "She must work in customer service?"

"Cain said that she's in Real Estate, why?"

"Oh, I just see a picture posted a few days ago with her surrounded by co-workers inside of her office, I guess. She is the one sitting behind the desk blowing out her birthday candles."

"Yea, she's a lil businesswoman and got me by about 2 years in age. So, I think she's about 35 years old. I can't lie, she's a pretty woman, so I can see why Cain would sleep with her. However, I don't care who she is. He had no business fucking with nobody else on that level."

"I feel you," Tiana agreed. "Well, he makes some beautiful children. His daughter is so adorable with those bright eyes and curly hair. She ain't but 2 years old and got shoulder length ponytails already. Hell, I'm jealous." She joked.

"Shit, me too. But her mammi got long ass hair too, so she could take that from her side. That good shit, meaning those curls and baby edges that I'm so jealous of came from Cain's side, I'm sure. She looks just like Skylar to me. Skylar was a pretty girl."

"I only saw her a few times and she was a pretty girl. This baby definitely looks like her." Tiana chimed in. "Skylar was only nineteen when she was killed, right?"

"Yea, so young. Ironically, her death seems to be going unnoticed like Slick's death. Cain said that nobody is saying a thing about it."

"That's even weirder, especially because of the McCoy name. They have a lot of clout around here, something should come out sooner than later." Tiana said, while pouring her another glass of wine. "Well, but whatever came of Skylar's death?"

Lauren shrugged. "Who knows? You know I've been in that family over 12 years. I knew a lot about Skylar. She was not as good as most people thought she was."

"Meaning?"

"Meaning, she was a wild one. Hell, she was already indulging in alcohol and weed by the time she was 14. They always tried to put her on punishment because she was either not coming home at night or just out somewhere being grown. Notice I said, tried. Truth be told, she was just spoiled. Too spoiled if you ask me. They gave her too much. Her brothers praised her and always felt like she could do no wrong, even when she'd done wrong."

"Wow, I didn't know that."

"She was nice, so don't think I'm saying that. As a matter of fact, she was one of the sweetest people I knew; she just had a wild side. It reminds of something I used to hear Jah say. *Everybody has their virtues and vices.*"

"He's right." Tiana said with a slight smile.

"She definitely lived in the fast lane. Hell, she loved challenging nigga's to race her, but most of 'em wouldn't because of her gender. But, I'd heard how she spanked a few asses during a few street races. Of course, Cain would brag about it, but they never told their father because they knew he wouldn't have approved. The last thing he wanted was for her to become a street outlaw."

"Maybe that shit is just in their bloodline. All of 'em like fast cars, even though Jah is the only one that took after his dad."

"Yea, but the other 2 races, too. Just not like Jah. They do it more for recreational fun. Jah does it for his reputation and his respect in the streets."

"I just can't believe it's been 7 years, and nobody still knows nothing." Tiana chimed in, as she drank from her glass of wine.

"Speculations that her boyfriend did it was heavy in the streets, but I wasn't sold on that. He was a wild one himself. I'd met him a few times when he'd come around with her. He seemed to really be feeling her. He didn't look like the type that would blow her brains out. On top of that, forensics showed that she was pregnant."

"Whaaaat?!" Tiana asked, the tea was starting to heat up.

"Yea, people don't know that. The McCoy's kept all kinds of secrets when it came to her death."

"Like maybe the secret of what happened to Skylar's boyfriend." Tiana pondered with a curious expression.

"Girl, I don't wanna speak on that subject. Suddenly, I feel like somebody is listening to me." She said, while looking around like she'd gotten scared. "You know, snitches get stiches bitch."

Tiana grinned. "Girl stop. Ain't nobody in here."

"I know, just messing with you. But, still, you won't ever hear them talking about that. I've wanted to ask Cain over the years, but he won't even talk about it. He tells me not to talk about it too."

"Damn, it is serious."

"What makes this thing even more serious to me is that I heard she was fucking somebody else. Supposedly a married man."

"Noooooo," Tiana let out with surprised eyes. "You got to be kidding me."

"I wish I was. I'm not saying that part is true, but that's another thing they don't talk about either. And sadly, because her boyfriend was estranged from his family, nobody has really come forward to make it a big deal that he's gone."

"Damn, that's crazy. Did he disappear right after?"

"No, it was about 2 years after they found Skylar. I think about 2 years." She said with a perplexed expression. "Either way, it was a while after the fact."

"So, that's probably why Biggs and his crew were cleared." Tiana stated.

"According to his mom, he'd been having a hard time following Skylar's death and the last she knew he'd gotten on a bus leaving the city and said he was never coming back. He had no reason to stay. However, it's been 7 years and he still ain't came back."

"That's one of those story's that should be on 60 minutes." Tiana uttered.

"It's definitely an unsolved mystery. For all I know, he could be alive and well, and probably moved on with somebody." She shrugged. "Who knows?"

"You're right. Who knows?"

Lauren glanced down at the display screen of her cell phone. It's almost past 9. "I wonder how long Cain planning on keeping the baby out." She pondered.

"Ooooh, look at you being a good stepmom."

"Don't push it, T." Lauren uttered, as Tiana laughed out loud. "I'm gonna take my ass on home. I need to wash up and get myself together, so I can be prepared for tonight's company." She said, speaking of the little one.

"You straight? You can drive? You know me, I'll call your ass an Uber in a minute."

Lauren laughed. "I know you will. I'm straight. I do feel good though, but I'm not drunk, just a lil tipsy. It ain't like you live that far from me."

Tiana stood up to walk her sister to the door.

"What are you getting into tonight?" Lauren pondered.

"Not a damn thang. I'm gon' take my tipsy ass to sleep." She teased.

"You never know, Jah might hit you up tonight." Lauren teased.

"Girl, if he do I ain't even responding," she laughed.

"Yea, right."

"I betcha!"

"Whatever," Lauren chuckled. As she headed out to her car, Tiana closed the door behind her.

"Jabari's ass done went ghost since I know about his baby now." Tiana said to herself. Instead of going to bed like she'd told Lauren, she poured another glass of wine and headed into the bathroom where she ran a tub full of warm bubbly water. She sat her glass and her phone down by the tub, and then instantly came out of her clothes. She dipped her hand in the water to feel the temperature and with a satisfied smile, she got in. As she relaxed her head back on a towel, her phone chirped of an incoming message. She reached over on the side of the tub and dried her hands, while picking her cell phone up to check it.

If I'm still blocked I'm just gonna assume you want me to come over there. You know I'll come. KORY

Tiana rolled her eyes. "You better not bring yo' ass over here." She uttered, while shaking her head. "He better not come."

By: Tiece

Ok!! so you ain't gon' respond back. KORY
"He so stupid." She mumbled.
Don't bring your ass over my house. TIANA
Now she responds. KORY
I said what I said. TIANA
I'm sorry Babe. I won't act like a jackass no more. I know I be fucking up but it ain't intentional. KORY
I really don't wanna hear this tonight. I'm getting ready for bed. TIANA
Damn, it's been a while since I saw you. KORY
That's what happens when people break up and go their separate ways. TIANA
Well, I miss you. KORY
Ok. Have a good night. TIANA
She sat her phone back down not wanting to be bothered. Relaxing her head back on the towel, she let out a deep breath while closing her eyes. The water soaking her skin was warm and tranquil, as she enjoyed the moment. Her phone chirped again, interrupting her peaceful thoughts.

"Damn," she let out. She grabbed the phone ready to let Kory have it this time, but before opening the message she noticed it was Jabari texting. Quickly, she read it.

Can we talk? I feel the need to explain some things to you. Are you busy tonight? I wanna come over. JAH

"Oh, now you wanna talk? Better yet, you wanna come over?" Tiana pondered to herself. "I'm not responding back. Tiana don't you respond back." She coached herself.

The only thing she wanted to do was forget about Kory and Jabari. What she needed was a calm night of peaceful thinking without the drama, the secrets or the headaches. For that matter, she didn't care for the company, either. And even though it all sounded good, that shit would have to wait for another night.

Sure, you can come over. TIANA

Chapter Seven

Tiana opened the door up to Jabari standing there with a handsome smile on his face. "Wassup Sexy." The tone of his voice turned her on.

He quickly glanced her over, enjoying his view of her wearing a simple white pair of boy shorts and a fitted white tank top.

"Hey you," Tiana spoke back with a frown. "Come in. You want something to drink? I was just sipping on this red wine."

"Red wine huh?" he grinned. "Yea, let me get some of that red wine."

Tiana stepped into the kitchen with Jabari right behind her. "You sure?" she laughed. "I have beer and some Hennessy. You don't have to drink what I'm drinking."

"I know, but I still want some of your wine. You ain't tryna renege now are you?" he joked. "Don't want your boy to taste none of your wine?"

Tiana laughed. "Noooooo, I was just saying." She said, as she grabbed a wine glass out the cabinet. "So, you'll be drinking out of a wine glass tonight sir."

"Okay," Jabari grinned. "I enjoy doing different things from time to time.

Tiana poured him up a glass of the good stuff and then escorted him to her bedroom. Jabari instantly pulled his shoes off.

"Oh, you're getting comfortable I see."

"Shit, you got me drinking wine tonight, I might as well." He teased.

"I don't mind," Tiana assured him with a cute smile, as she sat on her bed.

"Don't think I'm getting in this bed to have sex with you tonight."

Tiana laughed out loud. "Oh, really?" she thought that was the cutest lie ever.

"I'm for real." He laughed, and then drank from his glass of wine. "This shit good."

"Oh, yeah I meant to warn you. You might get hooked on it because it's just that good."

Jabari grinned. "I don't know about that." He clowned. "But, it is good."

They sat in the bed next to each other, both with their backs against pillows, as the sultry sounds of Prince played in the background.

"I appreciate you allowing me to come over." He said.

"Well, I figured we had a few things to talk about. So, why not," she shrugged, and then took a sip.

"So, you wanna get some shit off yo' chest too?"

"Yea," she responded. "If you're gonna be honest about what you have going on then I should let you in on a few things too."

Jabari drank a little. "Well, I'm all ears." He said.

"Oh, you don't wanna go first?" she grinned.

"Okay, let me see where I should start."

"Start with telling me about your relationship and the baby." Tiana told him, as she stared in his face.

"I'm not in a relationship, let's be clear on that. However, I was still visiting Cashmere from time to time. Not only is the sex good, but she was good to me when I was locked up."

Tiana sipped from her wine and continued to listen. She knew they were still having sex because Cashmere was pregnant and saying he was the daddy.

"I don't wanna lie to you about nothing. I think the more we're on the same page the better it will be."

"I agree." Tiana said.

"Cashmere is a cool girl and I've known her for about six years. However, while I was gone I feel like she was fucking around. I don't wanna go into any reasons or nothing like that. Eventually, I just decided it was best for us to go our separate ways."

"Damn, so you did it like that? What if she wasn't messing around?"

"I'll ask for forgiveness if I'm wrong. The truth will come to the light."

"How do you propose that?" Tiana pondered.

"The baby." He responded.

Tiana frowned. "The baby?"

"Yea, see I prayed for a sign. I prayed for answers, so I'd know I'm not making the wrong decision. Her getting pregnant wasn't something I expected, because she's been on the pill for years. But, now I take it as a sign. If the baby is mine—"

Tiana cut in. "It gives you another reason to stay, and maybe you were wrong about her."

Jabari shrugged. "Yea, maybe." He responded, just wanting to keep it as 100 as he could. "But if the baby ain't mine, then that tells me she's been crooked for a while."

"So, would you move on if the baby ain't yours?"

"Hell, yea, but I don't want you to think that I'm having thoughts of staying with her, either way. I don't know." He shook his head. "It's a lot of stuff I don't know now, but what I do know is if that baby ain't mine, it's a wrap."

"Got it," Tiana said. She didn't know if she quite understood it all, but she'd try to comprehend as much as could and take it for whatever it presented itself as.

"So, what's up with you? What you got going on?"

"Weeell," Tiana stalled.

"Nah, you can't be reneging." He joked.

"I'm not," she laughed. "I'm also not in a relationship and I guess I'm not really looking to be in one, either. If it happens, it happens. If it don't, no biggie."

"No biggie, huh?" he pondered, trying to feel her out.

"Nope," she responded.

"I do have an Ex that still hits me up from time to time. However, we're not together. I have a best friend that has been my best friend, since Jesus was a baby and well—"

"Well what?" Jabari asked with curious eyes.

"She's bisexual, more into women than men though. I believe she's fully gay, she just don't wanna admit it." She grinned. "Anyway, one drunken night our senior year in high school led to a passionate kiss between us. Let's just say after that, we kicked it from time to time over the years."

Jabari's eyes stretched open as he intently listened.

"Not like that." Tiana said, to calm him down. "It doesn't happen often, but it has happened."

"So, what you mean by that? Y'all have threesomes or is it just you and her?"

"It's mostly just me and her. However, we've had an audience before."

"An audience?"

"Meaning my boyfriend watching." She explained.

"Ohhh okay."

"But still it's always just me and her." She assured him.

"Damn," Jabari uttered, while trying to tame an aroused erection.

"Oh, so you getting off on this?" Tiana laughed out loud.

"Hell, yea. What straight nigga wouldn't be?" he clowned, but was very serious.

"I just wanted to be completely honest with you."

"And I'm loving your honesty." He grinned while enjoying their conversation. He liked the fact that she was open and honest with him. Most women wouldn't be so candid.

"My daughter's father is also in the picture, but not like that. He drives trucks and is hardly around. We're just cool parents and that works for us."

"I feel you."

"Look, I like you. I'm really feeling what we have, but I ain't expecting nothing. So, I don't want you to think that just because you're here I'm labeling what we have. My grandmother always told me to have a heart, but don't have no feelings."

"Wow, that's funny because Slick used to say that all the time too. Have a heart, but don't have no feelings." He reminisced.

"Yea, them feelings will get you fucked up; especially if they're not mutual. So, that's why I wanted to explain that to you. We're good and if it's meant for something more to pop off between us then it will."

Jabari smiled. "I like the way you think."

"So, I'm glad we've gotten that out the way."

"Me too. The conversation was quite enlightening." He said. "This wine got me talking all proper and shit."

Tiana laughed out loud. "I hear you."

"So, hear this and let me taste them sweet lips." He smiled, while licking his lips.

"Shiiiiid you ain't said nothing," she responded with a sexy grin, and then leaned over and kissed him. Jabari was definitely feeling the vibe as he kissed her back. He started to come out of his shirt, but something caught the corner of his eye. He looked up and noticed someone peeking through the window.

"What the FUCK?!" He jumped to his feet, as Tiana hurriedly hopped up out the bed behind him.

"WHAT?!" She frantically questioned.

"Somebody was at your window." He said, while at the same time slipping his shoes back on.

Tiana frowned. "At my window?" Just that fast loud knocking could be heard banging on her front door.

"Open the fucking door Tiana! I know you in there with a nigga!" Kory yelled out.

"Ah shit, that's Kory." She nervously said.

"Kory? Is that your ex or SUPPOSED to be ex?" Jabari questioned with a scowl on his face.

"Yea, that's my EX," she emphasized. "I don't know what he's doing here acting stupid and peeking in windows for. He knows it's over with us." Tiana explained, as she headed for the front door.

"Don't sound like it." Jabari uttered, as the loud banging on the front door continued. He simply followed Tiana.

"He's a whole mess outside with his dumb ass." She said.

"You gon' let the nigga in?"

"I'm gon' call the police on his ass if he don't leave." Tiana responded. "He's not welcome here. I been told him that."

"Some nigga's don't get the picture." Jabari uttered, just as they approached the front door.

"Kory, why the hell are you at my house?" Tiana asked through the door.

"I came to see you and you in there laid up with another nigga." Kory yelled out.

Tiana looked over at Jabari. "He's been drinking." She told him with a shake of the head. "Kory it's over! What part of that don't you understand?"

"I don't understand how you move the fuck on so fast!" he yelled in anger. "You fucking slut ass bitch!"

"Open the door. I'm gon' knock his drunk ass out." Jabari said. He was already tired of Kory's big, disrespectful mouth.

"Kory, I'm gon' call the police if you don't leave!" Tiana yelled out. "You're drunk and you're acting foolish! I need you to get off my property!"

"I ain't going nowhere bitch! You all hoc'd up with another nigga. I'll knock his bitch ass out! Open the fucking door right now or I'm gon' kick the bitch down."

"Open the door." Jabari insisted.

"No," Tiana softly said with a shake of the head. The last thing she wanted was for them to be fighting and over nothing. She knew it was over with her and Kory, he just was acting like he had amnesia. "Just wait, he'll leave."

"He must do this shit all the time?"

"He's never done this before."

"Not that you know of, because that nigga been peeping in yo' windows." Jabari explained, just as the doorknob began to rattle like Kory was trying to come in. "Open the door right now!"

"No, he'll leave."

By: Tiece

"Come on, just open the door." Jabari said in a firmer tone.

Tiana simply shook her head in defeat, while slowly opening the door. The minute it was wide enough for Kory to fit his arm in he grabbed Tiana by the throat. Jabari came from behind her and cold cocked his ass. A one hitter quitter knocked Kory straight out on Tiana's front porch. Instantly, he started snoring.

"Oh SHIT!" Tiana let out. "Is he okay?!"

Jabari glanced down at him. "His pussy ass a'ight." He responded. "Come on, let's get out of here."

Tiana frowned. "And just leave him like this?"

"Yep," Jabari answered, as he headed for his car. Once opening the driver door, he glanced back at Tiana again. "You coming?"

Tiana looked down at Kory, and then back out at Jabari. "Hold up, let me grab my purse."

"Lock the door up behind you." Jabari smugly grinned. He was most liked for his charming ways, but more respected as a street outlaw. It was also nothing for him to knock a nigga out. He'd done it at least three times in his life, but all three niggas deserved it. If push came to shove, he'd fight and that's why most people didn't fuck with him. However, Kory didn't know any better and had to learn the hard way.

Chapter Eight

It was Sunday around noon and Jabari was still laying around in bed. His thoughts were all over the place. He could never fully shake losing Slick or his sister. It was always a constant reminder in the back of his mind, no matter how much he tried to avoid it. He thought about some of their last conversations they'd had. He felt bad that he didn't get to leave any heirs to carry on his name or that he wouldn't be around to meet his baby. It was so much that had happened since the day he left. There was so much that he was still mad about and couldn't let go. As he lay there taking in deep breath and then letting it out, his cell phone rang. He reached over on the nightstand to answer it.

"Wassup scary cat." He clowned.

"When are you gonna stop calling me that? I couldn't just leave the nigga knocked out on my porch." Tiana laughed. "What if we had gotten back and he had croaked?"

"Oh well," Jabari joked. "He shouldn't have been fucking around at your house that time of night acting like a damn fool."

"You got that part right." Tiana agreed. "When his ass awakened, he got up and dipped. I still ain't heard from that nigga since."

Jabari laughed. "You should be thanking me then."

"Thank you sir." Tiana grinned. "I can't even look at his ass the same no more."

"Good, my job is done."

"Oh no it's not." Tiana chimed in.

"Not with you, Babe. It's with his punk ass. You didn't need a nigga like him, anyway. I didn't like the names he was calling you. Showed me that the nigga real disrespectful with a foul ass mouth. I wanted nothing more than to close it shut for a few days. Give him time to think about how foolish he was acting."

"You definitely had that mouth closed for a few days. His sister called me and said his lip was busted so bad that he could hardly talk. How the hell you did that with one lick?"

Jabari shrugged like she could see him. "I don't know." He responded. "But what you should know is I ain't never hit a nigga that didn't deserve it."

"I believe you." Tiana uttered. "So, what are you doing? Are you getting ready for the race this evening?"

"I'm still laying down."

"You what? When do you plan on getting up?"

"Soon, I just have a few things on my mind. Tonight, I'm dedicating the race to Slick. I know he'll be there in spirit and cheering me on. I almost don't wanna race just because he won't be there in the flesh, but he wouldn't want that."

"Awww, that's sweet. And you're right, he definitely wouldn't want that. I don't know him, but I could tell that y'all had a close relationship from the times I've seen y'all hanging out at the track."

"Yea, that was my nigga. Will you be coming tonight?"

Of course, I will. I'm gonna always support you, even during the times when I can't come through."

"Well, I appreciate that." Jabari responded with a smile. "What are you— Hold up, my brother beeping in. Matter of fact, I'm gon' hit you back later."

"Okay, you're fine. Handle your business."

"A'ight Babe." Jabari said, and then ended that call, but started another one. "Wassup Bruh."

"What you doing B?" Cain asked. "Sound like you still sleep."

"I ain't sleep, but I ain't out the bed either."

"What you waiting on? You need to be getting your day started."

"I know. I'll be getting up in a lil bit." Jabari told him.

"Pops want us to meet him at the shop by 5 this afternoon."

"Who is us?" Jabari pondered.

"You, Unc, Justin, Bruno and me." Cain answered.

"Oh, okay. Well, I'll be getting up in a lil bit." He said, stretching his arms out and yawning.

"You still got time, but you don't need to be wasting too much time. We need you ready for the race. The only thing we know about this dude is he's 23 years old with 9 wins, no losses. I've watched his YouTube channel a few times and he's arrogant as fuck. Much worse than you were at that age."

"Hush nigga." Jabari laughed.

"For real. Cat got a mouth full of gold, dreads down his back, tattoos all over including on his face—"

"Yea, I've watched some of those videos." Jabari grinned. "Homeboy be wildn', but he seems cool as fuck. He likes flashing his Rolex on camera. I guess that's his good luck charm."

"It is, at least that's what he be saying." Cain laughed. "He's been trying to set this race up since you first came home. The nigga really wanna race you."

"Who don't wanna race me right about now? These niggas got stock that's going up because they fucking with me. Niggas coming out of nowhere wanting to get some of this smoke. First two races back and I won. Technically, I'm on a winning spree again, but this time ain't nobody gonna break it. Stunner... That's his name right?"

"Yea, they call him Stunner, like he's the number 1 Stunner." Cain chuckled.

"That nigga do be stuntin' though. Flashing them gold teeth and his Gucci gear from head to toe. He love dancing around with bands in his hands." Jabari joked, but was dead serious.

"He got the right name, that's for sure." Cain continued to laugh.

"Exactly," Jabari agreed. "Homeboy lucky though. If he wasn't putting up 15 bands to race me, I wouldn't even do it. He ain't got enough wins for me, but hey. I'm gon' take his bread and losing still gon' put him in the spotlight. It's a win, win across the board."

"You got that right. The spotlight is all he wants anyway." Cain agreed.

"So, stop by the crib and pick me up. I'm gon' ride with you to the shop."

"That'll work." Jabari responded. "Well, let me get showered up and shit. I'll text when I'm leaving."

"A'ight B," Cain said, and with that they ended their call.

Jabari sluggishly got out of bed and then headed for the bathroom to shower. He had a long day ahead of him and an exciting night to follow. A part of him was just as amped as Stunner was. More than anything he just got a thrill out of winning and tonight would be no different.

Jabari pulled up to the shop, as he looked over at Cain. "Wake yo' ass up nigga. What's wrong with you?"

Cain cracked his eyes. "Damn, we here already?"

"Hell yea. You dozed off the minute you got in the car. You ain't getting no sleep Bruh?"

"Hell nawl," Cain responded. "Lauren been keeping my ass up all night. I'm talking about ever since I bought Cannon home, she's changed."

"Changed how?"

"Boy she been fucking the hell outta me."

Jabari laughed. "Lauren ain't no slow leak. She knows what time it is."

"I didn't even keep him that night. I ended up taking him back home. I did tell her she could ride with me, so she wouldn't be thinking nothing."

"Well, that was good."

"But aye Bruh, on the way back from dropping my boy off, she sucked my dick till we pulled back up in our driveway."

"Damn, Lauren doing it like that?" Jabari grinned. "That's right Sis, step yo' game up."

Cain laughed. "I don't know what's gotten into her, but I like it."

"I bet you do." Jabari grinned.

"So, but what's going on with you and Tiana?"

"I like her," Jabari confessed. "I like her a lot. We talk."

"Talk, talk?"

Jabari shrugged, still evading the question. "We kick it."

"Nigga! Is y'all fucking or nah?" Cain pondered.

Jabari laughed out loud. "Yea, I guess you can say that."

"That's my brother," he smugly chuckled with an approving nod of the head. "I knew you'd hit it sooner or later."

"That's the thing, though. We only did it once and that was weeks ago." He said, not wanting to mention it happened the night Slick was killed. Even though that was one of the best nights he'd had, he still felt bad about not staying with Slick.

"Damn," Cain uttered. "It's you or her?"

"Mostly me." He admitted.

"Don't worry, it'll happen again. I mean, you've had a lot going on."

"You're right and she understands that. However, it would've happened a few nights ago, but I had to knock out some pussy ass ex-boyfriend of hers that was peeking through the damn window."

"What Bruh?!"

"You heard me. Her ex was caught peeking in her window, but instead of this nigga leaving once he'd been spotted, he goes to the front door and starts beating on it."

"What the fuck wrong with him? He must not be an ex, acting like that."

"She said they ain't fucking around no more, and I believe her. On the other hand, I can understand the nigga might be whipped. Shawty on her A-game across the board."

Cain grinned. "That sounds about right."

"Anyway, he was already outside talking crazy and calling her names. You know I ain't like that shit. I'm telling her to open the door. She nervous and shit, kept telling me no."

"Hell, she probably was scared."

"She was, but she knew she had to open the door or call the police. Finally, she opened the door and this nigga gon' reach in and try to choke her. I hit his ass so fast and knocked him out. Right there on her front porch."

Cain laughed out loud. "Damn, he didn't even know who knocked him out."

"It happened so fast, he probably thought she did it." They cracked up laughing, just as Justin exited the shop.

"What y'all nigga's out here laughing 'bout?" he asked.

Cain and Jabari got out of the car. "Yo' brother out here knocking cat's out." Cain chuckled.

"Damn, y'all gotta fill me in." He grinned. "But aye, Pops and Unc in there waiting."

"We're right behind you." Jabari said, as they followed Justin into the shop.

"So, what you're saying is that we need to watch everybody we hang around?" Cain pondered with a serious expression.

"Yea, basically." Biggs responded. "It's definitely something not right and I wish you had told me sooner about the last conversation y'all had." He said to Jabari.

"I know, but I was confused as to what he was talking about. He was so evasive." Jabari explained. "I do know he said that whatever he was looking into was close to home."

"You sure he didn't have any debt in the streets?" Justin asked.

"Nawl, I told you he didn't. I believed him. Slick had money, he was just quiet with it. He didn't have problems unless it had something to do with a bitch."

"That's it. We need to holla at everybody he was fucking and see if they know something." Justin said.

Papers nodded his head. "We're gonna get around to that. It's too soon. Hell, it ain't even been a month yet. Even if they were some side chicks, fuck buddy's or whatever Slick had it going on, I'm sure they're still grieving. Plus, it was a lot of women at that funeral falling out and crying."

"It was women there crying that I didn't even know," Jabari added.

"I think we all felt the same way." Cain joked, but was very serious. "Y'all know Slick had that pretty boy swag. The women couldn't resist him."

Jabari grinned with a nod of the head. "You got that right."

"So, what's next?" Bruno asked, as he'd sat there only listening. He didn't talk much unless it was about somebody's business. Business that could hurt anybody in the McCoy family. He was indebted to them and that would never change for nobody.

"Just lay low, hang around only those we trust, which are only the ones that are in this room. Don't get me wrong, we're still gonna handle business, carry on with the crew and work, but you can't afford to trust nobody. Whatever's said, pay close attention to it. I would hate to think it's somebody that close in our circle that could kill Slick and we not know who it is. That means they have access to any one of us."

"That's some scary shit." Bruno uttered with a shake of the head.

"Pops I know we aren't supposed to talk about this, but do you think it could have something to do with Skylar's death?"

"I'm glad somebody said it," Justin mumbled.

"Mars, the dude she was talking to skipped town about 2 years after her death. Even though he claimed he was innocent, was he? After all, he was the one that was coming out of the trailer that Skyler's body was found in. Do you think he's back and has us on his radar?"

"Nah," Papers intervened. "I highly doubt that." He assured him. However, Papers and Biggs knew where Mars was, but nobody else knew but them. Just in case the police questioned anybody other than them, they wouldn't detect a lie. Simply because they never planned on nobody else knowing about their secret.

"I was thinking the same thing. I mean, that could be a lot to deal with mentally; especially if he did it."

"But, why come for us? Skylar was one of us, so if he didn't kill her then we shouldn't be on his radar." Justin interrupted.

"He didn't like us though, because we didn't think he was good enough for our sister."

"Nobody was," Biggs uttered, as Cain continued.

"He was a lil hot head in the streets and portrayed a thug lifestyle. Maybe he couldn't stand the fact that we'd never accept him. That could be a reason why he did that shit. Maybe Skylar was leaving him. She could've been calling it off and he couldn't take it." He said, while looking over at Jabari. "What you think?"

Jabari shrugged. "I don't know what to think."

"Me either," Justin agreed.

"We don't even know if this has anything to do with Skylar though, right?" Bruno asked.

"We don't know, but we need to be aware of it if it is." Biggs responded. "I know we're gearing up for this race tonight, but keep your eyes open and your ears to the streets. It's something going on and it's right in our faces; we just didn't know it was anything worth seeing. Think about the last conversations we had with her. Think hard. See if anything stands out to you." He coached. "It's there."

"And, if this has nothing to do with Skylar then what?" Justin asked.

"Then still pay attention, either way something is going to stick out. Now that we may have an idea of where the hate is coming from, we can better handle the situation." Papers responded.

"I agree," Biggs chimed in.

Chapter Nine

"I thought y'all were finish working on my car?" Skylar asked, as she entered the shop.

"Your dad told me to check the brakes. So, that's all I'm doing." Bruno responded.

"Wassup Sis?" Cain spoke.

"Hey Bruh," Skylar said with a smile, as she walked over and put her arms around him. "It's been a minute since I've seen you. Where you been?"

"I've been hanging out here and home. I'll be going to Miami Beach next weekend. You know it's me and Lauren's 5th anniversary."

"Aww, isn't that sweet. You may as well marry her already."

"Nah, I don't think I'm ever getting married." Cain said with a shake of the head. "We're good for now, anyway."

"I hear you."

"Anyway, where you been? You're the one that's been M.I.A. lately."

"Mom and Dad are just exaggerating. They know where I be at." Skylar grinned. "But I told 'em I'm moving away soon and I'm only coming home to visit."

"Yea right. They wouldn't stand for that."

"I'll be 19 years old tomorrow. I can do whatever I wanna do." She responded. "Ain't that right Bruno?"

"My name Bess, I ain't in that mess." Bruno responded, as Skylar laughed. "It's okay. You're family now, you can take sides." She joked.

"So, I guess you and your lil knucklehead boyfriend gon' skip town together?"

"Who said he's my boyfriend?" she asked in a joking manner.

"Oh, that's yo' nigga. Ma said you be leaving the house and be gone all day long with him."

"Oh, did she?" Skyla shrugged. "Ma wish she knew what I was doing."

"Well, as long as it's not with him then you're good in my book." Cain told her, as he kissed her softly on the forehead. "Stay out of trouble. Ma and Pops worry about you. We all do."

"Don't worry about me. I got this." She laughed while playfully punching him in the stomach. "Y'all worry too much."

Bruno slid from under Skylar's car. "You're good to go."

"Okay good. So, I'll go tell Trish that she can leave. I'll be back." She said, walking off. "You gon' pull it outside for me?" she asked while glancing back over her shoulder.

"Yea, I'll do that." Bruno said.

"Well, I'm gon' get on outta here. Lauren is ovulating. We tryna go half on a baby."

Skylar was tickled. "Ayyye, I likes that. I think it's great that we're growing our family."

Cain smiled and hugged her once more. "See you later, Sis. Love you." He said with his arms wrapped tightly around her. What he didn't know was that would be his last time ever hugging her again.

"Bruh," Jabari called out again, snapping Cain back to reality. "Wassup? What you over there thinking about? I called you at least three times."

"My bad B. I was just thinking." He said. "Sorry 'bout that. Wassup?"

"Tonio just spanked Buddy's ass. That's what's up!" Jabari excitedly said.

"I saw it," Cain said with a pleasing smile. "I just had wandered off for a bit."

"Damn, that was a good race." Bruno chimed in. "Tonio almost lost it for a moment in the beginning."

"Yea, I saw that." Jabari said, "But he straightened up and jetted right past by Buddy so fast. One blink and you would've missed it."

"Right, cause all I caught was tail end of it." Cain uttered.

"Bruh, I'm gon' need you to pay attention." Jabari said with a shake of the head. "Bruno did you catch all that for YouTube?"

"Every bit of it." Bruno replied. "Cain, you see all these people out here tonight. The best is yet to come!"

"Yea, I can feel it in the air." Cain responded with a satisfied grin, while looking down at his cell phone to read an incoming text message. "I just got word that Stunner and his crew are about 45 minutes away."

"Okay, good." Jabari nodded. "That gives me time to go mingle a little. You know er' body wants to get a picture with The Goat." He teased, but wasn't playing.

Cain grinned, just as Justin walked up. "I'm walking with you, Bruh. I know it's some baddies out here tonight. Damn, who is that?" he asked, as Cain's eyes widened.

"That's Sofia, my baby mama."

"Oh damn. I see lil Cannon now." Justin said, noticing the female that was with Sofia holding the baby. "Who is that?"

"That's her sister." Jabari chimed in, as he admired how sexy Yolanda was. Suddenly, all eyes were on them as they made their way over, both speaking to the brothers as they joined them.

"Hey man," Cain said, as he reached for his son. "Why you bring him out here? It's a lot going on and it's about to get real loud when these races start."

Sofia reached inside Cannon's baby bag and pulled out a pair of Beats wireless headphones for kids. They were the Mickey's 90th anniversary edition.

Justin smiled. "Aye, I like that. Your headphones are nice nephew."

Jabari nodded an approving smile. "Yea, I like those."

"I just wanted him to see his uncle race tonight." Sofia said. "Ain't nothing wrong with that is it?"

Cain shook his head with a change of heart. "Nah, I'm actually glad he's here." He answered. He liked how his brothers were gushing over his son. He loved even more that Sofia was using his money in the way he intended. He didn't mind her buying a pair of $240.00 Beats for Cannon, as long as it was for Cannon. He admired his fit. The little one was rocking a red and black, button up Polo shirt and a pair of black Polo jeans. Cain looked down at his shoes. "My boy clean tonight." He said with a smile on his face, as he peeped the red and black pair of Jordon's on Cannon's feet. Ironically, Cannon was looking just like his daddy sporting a black and red fitted cap just big enough for his small, round head. For some reason, it was a proud moment for Cain until Lauren popped up.

"Hey," Lauren spoke, as she walked over. "Hey Cannon."

"Hey," Sofia spoke back. "Tell her hey Cannon."

Lauren put on a big, fake smile, as she stared at the baby. It was nothing against him, but she hated the fact that his mama could just show up anywhere with him and take all of Cain's attention."

Yolanda peeped the tension and reached for Cannon. "Hey," she said to Lauren. "Come on Nephew. Let's go sit in the stands and wait for mommy." She said.

"Hey," Lauren spoke back, but she could feel the tension in the air. It was thick as hell.

Cain stood there somewhat shocked as he handed Cannon over to his auntie. The minute he was in tow, she walked off. Jabari and Justin also took that as their queue to leave. Cain mentally took in a deep breath and held it in for a second. *Damn, this some crazy shit*, he thought, as he looked over at Lauren. "Wassup Bae?" he asked.

"Hey Baby. I just came over since I saw the little one out tonight." She said with an unbothered smile. "He's dressed so cute."

"Thanks," Sofia said, with an unnerved smile.

"Baby, do you mind if I speak to Sofia for a minute." She asked. Cain's eyes widened, as Sofia seemed a bit shocked.

"Why, you good?" Cain asked. He didn't know what to make out of her asking him that.

"Yea, I'm good. I just wanna make sure that she and I are good." She told him.

Cane stepped back. "Okaaaay," he said, as he slowly backed away. He wanted to make sure that no licks would be thrown just in case he needed to intervene.

Lauren looked Sofia up and down. She had on a professionally done lavender wig that actually looked good on her, and a lavender and white Nike short set. She glanced down at her shoes, smirking at the lavender and white Air Max on her feet.

"I see Cain is doing right by you and Cannon." Lauren started with a serious expression on her face.

"He is," Sofia shot back with a smile.

"I just need you to know that I have nothing against you and anytime Cannon comes around I'll treat him like my own. I also need you to know that Cain is my man and just because your baby mama number 2 doesn't mean that he's leaving me to be with you."

"Oh wow," Sofia said, while continuing to smile. "Bothered much?"

"Not bothered at all, just letting you know where I stand, so you'll know not to move out of your place." Lauren shot back. "Look at him." She said, glancing over her shoulder. "He looks good. I know it and being that you have a baby by him, we both know what he's working with—"

"Okay, and your point is?" Sofia asked.

"My point is that he's my man. You're his baby mama. He will always be there for his son and I'll never block that. But, he's not for you. Do we understand?"

"Babe?" Cain called out. "Y'all good?"

Lauren shot him a fake smile and then looked back over at Sofia. "Are we good?" she asked.

Sofia grinned, even though she was much younger she wasn't a fool. What Lauren may have wanted to get out of her wasn't going to happen. She wasn't about to step out of character nor was she going to tell her anything that wasn't her business. She knew how to play her cards right.

"Well?" Lauren asked again.

"Oh yea, we're good." She said. "Guess I'll go get my son. Look at him, looking just like his daddy." Sofia walked off. She was proud of the way she had handled herself.

By: Tiece

Lauren went in the opposite direction towards Cain. Once in close range she kissed him softly on the lips. Letting any bitch watching know that he was off limits.

"What's up, Sexy." Jabari said with a smile, as he and Tiana nearly bumped into each other. She was walking off from the concession stand just as he was going. "What you got there?"

"Just a bottled water and some cotton candy."

"Can I taste some of your cotton candy?" he asked with a wink.

Tiana blushed. "You can taste whatever you wanna taste."

He looked around. "Damn, it's too many people out here."

Tiana giggled.

"Oh, don't worry. I'm gonna remember that."

"I want you too." She told him.

As they were talking, Justin walked off to get him something to munch on.

"You seen my sister?" Tiana asked.

"Yea, she somewhere over there talking to Cain. She walked up on him and Sofia talking."

Lauren frowned. "Sofia's out here?"

"Yea, and she bought the baby."

"Oh wow."

"Lauren was cool though. I glanced a few times, as me and Bruh was walking off."

Tiana let out a deep breath. "Thank Goodness." She uttered. "Well, good luck tonight."

"I don't need luck, I have you." Jabari said.

"Oh, somebody got a lot of game tonight." She grinned, causing Jabari to laugh.

"Nah, no game over here."

"Hey! Let's take a picture with The Goat." A woman said to her girlfriends, as they walked over. "I hope we're not interrupting you, but can we please get a picture with you."

"Sure," Jabari nodded, as he smiled at Tiana and then waited for the ladies to get in formation for the picture.

"Who's gonna take it?" the lady asked.

Jabari glanced over his shoulder towards the concession stand. "Hold up, my brother is on the way back over—"

"I'll take it." Tiana cut in with a smile. She rather enjoyed seeing Jabari in this element. It made him even sexier to her.

Once the picture of taken, the ladies thanked him, flirted a little on the low, and then walked off.

"What you smiling about?" he asked Tiana.

"Oh, nothing." She responded, just as Justin walked back over.

"Well, I'm gonna let you two mix and mingle. I need to find my sister and make sure she's good."

"Yea, do that." Jabari said. "No good luck kiss tonight?"

Tiana looked over at him. "Really?"

"Yes, really."

Without hesitation, she leaned over and kissed him on the cheek. "How's that?"

"That's perfect." He smiled, as she turned to walk off. Jabari looked over at Justin. "Damn, I like her thick ass."

Justin grinned. "I can tell. Shawty is thick too."

"So, waddup?" Shyla spoke from behind, just as she walked up.

"Hey, what's going on?" Jabari asked. "Where's Cash?"

"You ain't talk to her?"

"Nah, not since earlier."

"Oh, she ain't feeling too good, so she sat this one out."

"Oh okay. I'm surprised she didn't tell me that."

"I'm sure she will." Shyla said, then focused her attention elsewhere. "Hey Justin." She blushed with a smile.

"Wassup," Justin spoke back. "How you doing? You looking good." He told her.

"Thanks," she responded, while admiring his straight white teeth and handsome smile.

"Who you here with?" he pondered.

"I have couple of cousins over there. I'll be joining them."

Justin nodded. "Oh okay."

"Well, I don't wanna hold y'all up. I'll see you around." She told him. "A'ight Jah. Good luck tonight."

"'Preciate that Shyla." He responded. She walked off in one direction, they walked off in the other. "She likes you Bruh."

Justin grinned. "I noticed."

The crowd was mad thick, as the brothers made their way back through it. Along the way, Jabari took a couple more photos with a few eager fans. The night was young, the air was a bit chill for it to be late August, but the wind blew about good vibes. It was a refreshing breeze that smelled like another win was coming their way.

"What's up with your boy?" Jabari asked, as they joined Cain and the crew.

"He's coming," Cain responded. A second later, the crowd suddenly grew silent as the loud, booming sounds of Encore by Jay Z was blaring in the background. "What the fuck?" Cain asked, as he looked towards the sound of the music.

Jabari and Justin laughed. "This nigga pulling up playing Encore by Jay Z."

The crew laughed.

"He funny as fuck." Justin chimed in.

"What he want an encore for? He 'bout to get his ass spanked." Cain clowned.

"This shit gon' be good." Bruno grinned, rubbing his hands together.

Clearly, the hype started when Stunner showed up. In true fashion, he was riding in a souped-up black Tahoe with 28' inch rims. Some of his crew was riding with him. They had the windows down and was crunk as hell. Behind him was a black 3500 Dodge Ram pulling a trailer that had his car in it. The crowd went crazy.

Jabari grinned with a shake of the head. "This nigga know he stuntin' tonight."

Justin agreed. "Hell yea, the crowd is loving this shit."

The crew stood back, talking and clowning amongst each other, as Stunner pulled up and parked. The minute he got out the SUV, people started surrounding him. He was definitely well known for his videos and wild antics.

"That nigga got his own camera crew following him around." Bruno said.

"That's why his YouTube channel be so hype. I mean, we got some good shit, but they have some really good shit." Justin said. They had a cameraman on call, but mostly for catching the events of them racing. However, Stunner's camerawoman followed him everywhere he went. So, in that aspect he was definitely more popular.

Stunner walked over to them and flashed his golden smile. His entire grill was gold. He had 3 Cuban gold chains around his neck, one with a lion medallion. On his wrists was a gold Rolex and on the other a glistening Cuban link bracelet. His gear was Gucci from head to toe, but his crew wore matching t-shirts that read, The #1 Stunner on the front and the number 10 in big block font on the back.

"Wassuuuup?" Stunner anxiously spoke, as he walked up.

"You," Jabari responded, as he reached out and shook his hand.

"I've been waiting for this moment." Stunner told him, as he looked around. "You bring out a crowd. I love it!"

"Nah, that's probably some of me and the rest for you."

Stunner smugly grinned and scoped the crowd again. "All this for me?"

"Why not?" Jabari coolly smiled.

Justin grinned. Jabari was always so smooth with it. He'd downplay his status to make his rival feel more important about himself, only to fall short in defeat in the end. It never failed. He definitely figured his brother would play this hand against an arrogant opponent like Stunner.

"So, what's the number 10 on the back of the shirts for? I thought you won 9 races." Jabari pondered.

"That 10 is for you." Stunner told him, as his crew laughed.

"Oh yea?" Jabari grinned, as his crew laughed.

"Y'all got jokes tonight." Cain cut in. "We gon' see who the real stunner is when the party over."

Stunner laughed out loud. "Yea, we gon' see."

"What you driving playboy?" Cain asked.

"Hold up. Yoooo, pull my baby out the trailer." Stunner instructed someone from his crew. "Where yo' ride at?"

"Pulling up now," Jabari responded, just as Biggs and Papers pulled up driving the all-white, F-450 Super Duty dually truck, transporting his race car in the back of the trailer.

"I love this shit!" Stunner exclaimed, as the crowd grew loud with anticipation. Just seeing the truck that carried Jabari's ride in it had everybody crunk.

Stunner's 1971 Chevelle S.S. pulled out of the trailer. The car was pearlescent painted with a black and orange blend. Painted flames covered the whole front part of the car, including most of the hood. The crowd went wild. The 540 big block under the hood was roaring like a lion ready for battle.

"That's sweet," Jabari told him.

"Yea, I know." Stunner responded with arrogance.

Cain nodded. "Yea, I like that." He added, admiring Stunner's car.

Papers pulled the indigo blue, 69 Camaro z28 off the trailer. Just like predicted, the people started cheering, *The Goat is back! The Goat is back! The Goat is back!*

By: Tiece

"Daaaaaamn, you got it like this?" Stunner questioned with a big smile on his face. "You getting this footage?" he asked his camerawoman.

"Indeed," she responded, while recording the hype people.

In no time, the cars were lined up on the track side by side, each in its own lane. The sound of the engines were loud and ready to rumble.

Jabari stood outside his car and threw up his lucky coin, landing on heads. He smiled as he looked over at his opponent. "This win is for you Slick." He kissed two fingers and raised his hand in the air. "I wish you could be here to see this shit." He joked.

Stunner was jumping up and down in front of the camera flexing his Rolex and flashing his gold grill. In a way it really tickled Jabari, as he grinned to himself. He then jumped in his car, zoning everything out around him. The only thing he saw was the strip leading to the winning line. He revved up his engine, showboating just a little bit, and when it was time to mash the gas he sped off like a rocket launching into outer space. Looking straight ahead with his eye on the prize, Jabari could feel his victory coming. A loud, explosive sound could be heard just as he crossed the finished line. He looked back to see that he had definitely won the race, but Stunner was nowhere close behind him. His car had backfired, coughing up smoke while stalling. Jabari grinned. Even if Stunner didn't have car problems the race was his. The triumphant win was everything, as he could hear the crowd chanting, *The Goat Is Back! The Goat Is Back! The Goat Is Back...* It was one of the best feelings in the world. He beamed inside while looking over like somebody was in the passenger seat. "That was for you my nigga." He said in memory of Slick.

Chapter Ten

"Hey you, Congratulations!"

"Thank you," Jabari responded. "I was looking for you after the race. You good?"

"Yea, I'm straight. I had to leave right after you won because I needed to take my daughter to the ER."

"Oh damn, is she okay?"

"Yea she stabbed her finger trying to take her braids out. We're in one of the rooms now. They just gave her 9 stiches."

"Damn, that's crazy. Sounds like it hurts too."

"Oh yea, she scared me so bad with all that crying. I guess she was in a lot of pain."

"Mommy, I was," the soft voice said in the background. "I'm glad they gave me that shot."

"I am too, because that calmed you down." Tiana said to her daughter.

"Well, I'm glad she's better." Jabari eased in. "You wanna just hit me up tomorrow then?"

"Damn, I really wanted to see you."

"I know. I wanted to see you too."

"It's been weeks since we last—" she paused, as she looked over at her daughter. "Well, um."

Jabari laughed. "Yea, it's been weeks, but it's okay. It's coming again and when it do, I'm making up for the old and the new."

Tiana giggled. "You better. How are you feeling? You kicked ass tonight and I loved it."

Jabari grinned. "I feel good. I hate that Slick ain't here in the flesh to see it, but I know he was here in spirit."

"He was definitely there cheering you on."

"I know. How long you think you'll be there?"

"I'm not sure. It shouldn't be that much longer. What are you going to be doing tonight?"

"Justin asked me to go to Club Two with him and the crew tonight, but I'm not with that type of crowd. However, call me if you get a chance. The only way I don't answer is if I go home and fall asleep." He told her.

"Okay, I will." Tiana responded. "The doctor just stepped back in the room. We'll talk later."

"A'ight," Jabari said, and then they ended their call. As he drove the ride back from the track, thoughts of Cashmere crossed his mind. For as long as they'd been together she never missed a race. He called her. On the second ring she answered.

"Wassup Jah?" she said in the phone.

"You sound like you were knocked out. You okay over there?"

"Not really. This baby be having my ass sick all time of the day and night. I just laid down from throwing up." She explained. "I've been queasy since the time I woke up. Can't keep nothing down."

"Damn, I hate to hear that." Jabari sincerely responded.

"I hate to feel like this, but I'm good. Anyway, congratulations on your win tonight."

Jabari smiled. "Thanks."

"You know Shyla had called me on FaceTime so I could see it."

"That was cool of her to do."

"Yea, it wasn't the same as being there, but I was cheering you on from my bed." She teased.

"Thanks, that meant a lot." He told her. It was things like this that made him love her. She had her good ways and they'd for sure had a lot of good times. Now their love was being tested. He just didn't know if she'd pass or not. "Well, hey, while I'm out I can bring you something. If that's cool."

"Something like—"

"What you need? Graham crackers, saltine crackers, pickles, Ginger Ale?" he pondered. "Just something to help you feel better."

"Well, now that you mentioned it, you can bring me some saltine crackers and Ginger Ale. I just drank the last of my Ginger Ale tonight."

"Okay, cool. I'm gonna stop by the store and then I'll come by."

"Okay, I'll unlock the front door now, so you can just come on in when you get here."

"A'ight." Jabari said, and with that they ended their call. He drove in the direction of the nearest store. His cell phone rang.

"Wassup Bruh?"

"Wassup B. You good?" Cain asked.

"Yea, I'm 'bout to stop to the store shortly and grab Cashmere something for her nausea."

"Oh, okay. I thought you were hooking up with Tiana?"

"I was, but she had a slight emergency with her daughter. Everything is fine now, but she had to handle her business."

"I feel you."

"So, I was just out and thought about Cashmere. She has never missed one of my races, but she missed tonight. I knew she had to be sick, sick not to show up and support me."

"And, you're going over to try and help her feel better. You gon' pump some of that venom in her. Get her back right?" Cain teased.

"Niggaaa!" Jabari laughed. "Nah, I have no intentions of having sex with her. I'm just gon' go by, sit with her for a little while and leave. I told Tiana to call me anyway when she gets situated."

"I understand." Cain grinned. "But hey, just because you're feeling a ways about Cashmere doesn't mean you can't have some type of relationship with her. I mean, relations too." He added. "She knows you're living as a single man now, whether she's pregnant or not. She knows what the deal is. If I was you, I'd just be living Bruh. Enjoy this time of being a single man. One thing I will say off top is don't lie to 'em. I don't care how bad you think it'll make 'em feel. Just keep it 100. Trust me, a woman will respect that, and they'll keep you around. No matter what you got going on. You're king, Bruh. You can live like one if your heart desired."

"Look at you, my nigga speaking Shakespearian language and shit."

Cain grinned. "You better take heed lil Bruh. I get myself caught up because I be lying. I don't like hurting Lauren, so I'll lie. However, we've always been in a relationship. I didn't have a chance to live like you do now. You have that opportunity, take advantage of it. Actually, you living like Slick. I know he's looking down proud of this moment." He joked but was also serious.

Jabari pulled into an empty parking spot in front of the store. "You're right Bruh. You're absolutely right."

"At this point, you're entitled to live vicariously however the hell you want to. You got your own place and you can very well talk to whomever you want to, when you want to. Shit, I'm a lil jelly." Cain joked with laughter.

"You should be," Jabari laughed.

"Anyway, I'm gon' hit up Club Two with Justin for a little while then I'm going home. Lauren sending nude pics and shit. Getting my dick hard as a rock," he added, as Jabari laughed. He could hear Justin in the background laughing too.

"Yea, Bruh he 'bout to get kicked out over here making love to his phone." Justin said out loud.

Jabari laughed. "Man, y'all crazy as hell."

"Shit, I might tell his ass to drop me off first." Cain said.

"He lying." Justin said. "You know how he do. He need to go watch these strippers first, then he'll go home and lay it down."

"You know what to say Bruh. They get me even hyper. Plus, I need a few more drinks in my system because it's gon' be a long night. I just popped a Percocet too."

Justin and Jabari laughed. Cain always had a way of entertaining them. As he sat there clowning around with them, he looked up to see a familiar face coming out the store.

"Oh shit, I gotta go." He said.

"You good?" Cain asked.

"Yea," he assured him. "I'll hit y'all back."

"A'ight Bruh." Cain said, and then they ended their call.

"Aye, wassup?" Jabari said, as he got out of his car.

"Heyyy," Yolanda spoke with a bright smile. "What you doing here?"

"Your energy must've pulled me in this direction."

Yolanda was tickled. "Oh yea. My energy is that strong?"

Jabari handsomely smiled. "Must be." He answered.

"Soooo, what you getting into tonight?"

"Nothing much. What about you?" he pondered.

"I'll be going home tonight. My sister is going out. She's actually getting dressed at my house, so I'll be keeping my nephew for her."

"Oh okay. You're a really good auntie. Do you have any kids?"

"Not unless you wanna say that Cannon is mine." She joked.

"That's why I said you're a good auntie." Jabari laughed. "I'm glad my nephew has someone like you in his life. Not saying his mama is bad."

"I know what you're saying." She said just as her cell phone beeped of an incoming text message. She glanced down to read it.

What time you getting here? I'm dressed and ready to leave. SOFIA

Sit your thot ass down somewhere. I'm coming. YOLANDA

Lol Hush SOFIA

Yolanda looked up at Jabari, as she laughed a little. "That's her rushing me now." She told him.

Jabari nodded his head. "I figured," he said.

"Well, is it cool if I get your number? I mean, maybe we can talk sometimes. Well, unless you're in a committed relationship or something." She said all in one breath.

Jabari grinned. "Yea, you can get my number and no I'm not in a committed relationship."

Yolanda smiled from ear to ear. "Cool," she said, as she and Jabari exchanged numbers. They hugged each other for a brief second, and then parted ways. Jabari walked in the store with a satisfied smile on his face, definitely feeling like the man.

"Jah, that's you?" Cashmere called out from the bedroom.

"Yea," Jabari answered, as he made his way down the narrow hallway and into her bedroom. "You gon' get up? Want to me to fix you some of this Ginger Ale?" he asked.

"Yes, please," she responded.

In minutes, Jabari was back with Cashmere's glass of Ginger Ale. He handed her the saltine crackers too.

"Sit down," she told her. "I don't bite."

"I would hope not." He grinned, while sitting down on the other side of the bed. "Can I take my shoes off?"

Cashmere frowned. "You don't have to ask me that." She told him.

"I just wanna make sure." He said, while taking his shoes off. "You know I like to get comfortable."

"I know." She grinned. "That definitely hasn't changed."

"Well, speaking of change, I see that you've changed your room around. I see you have new living room furniture too. What you got going on?"

"I just wanted a change. And, as for the living room furniture, I actually got that out of Shyla's entertainment room. It looks new because no one is allowed in that room. However, Rich surprised her with a new living sectional that he says came from some Country and so, she asked if I wanted her old one." She explained.

"I like it. It's nice. So, that's what men buy now? Furniture from other Countries? Is that the key to a woman's heart now?"

Cashmere grinned, as she sipped from her Ginger Ale.

"Have I been gone that long?" he joked.

"No, you haven't." She laughed. "But, I don't know what Rich has going on. I think he's only buying stuff to put in her house, so it seems like he's actually living there or is a part of whatever this new life he has going on."

"What you mean by that?"

"Well, you know he moved to the West Coast and he supposed to be back and forth, living there with his family, and then being with Shyla when he's here. However, lately he has not been doing as he should be. At least, he's not spending any time with Shyla. Honestly, I don't think that Rich is into Shyla like that no more. I mean, he's going to always take care of her because of River and Ryder—"

"But, you don't feel like he wants to be with Shyla no more."

Cashmere shrugged.

"The man just bought her new furniture from another Country." He teased. "It's something there."

Cashmere laughed. "You got jokes," she clowned. "No, but he probably only got that furniture because Shyla was tripping. She said they argued to a point where she told him that she was calling it off and moving on with another nigga. Guess Rich didn't like that too hot. So, he called himself stepping up—"

"With furniture?" Jabari grinned. "That's funny."

"I agree." Cashmere laughed. "He's clearly full of shit. I don't know what that was about, but he was definitely trying to get on her good side."

"I'm sure." Jabari said. He looked over at Cashmere. She was beautiful with no make-up, skin just flawless. She had a beautiful smile and a good heart for the most part. He'd seen all sides of her which is how he knew that something was off the minute he touched down. However, now wasn't the time for him to even be thinking about that. He'd just won a race and was sitting on cloud nine. The only thing he was focused on was mending some type of relationship with Cashmere for the sake of the baby.

"So, how do you feel to be back on this winning spree?"

"It feels good. It brings back memories and reminds me of why I love racing. It's just in my blood."

"I agree," Cashmere said. "It was so many people out there tonight. A part of me was glad that I was home in bed. Even though I wished I could've been there for you."

Jabari smiled. "It's cool. I totally understand. The kid has you messed up right now."

"Yes, the kid does." Cashmere grinned.

"Cain's son was out there tonight. The baby mama bought him."

"Oh, that's wassup. I've seen him on social media. He's too cute. Looks just like a McCoy."

"He definitely looks just like his father."

"That would include all of y'all." Cashmere told him. "The whole damn family looks alike." She teased.

"That's what they say." He chuckled.

"I'm surprised she would take him to the track with all that noise. It be so fucking loud out there. Much too loud for a baby."

"Oh, he was prepared. She had him a pair of Beats?"

"For kids? They make those?"

"Yea, apparently they do and yea they fit him perfectly." He told her. "Lil fella was a part of my good luck tonight. I enjoyed seeing him out there. Makes me think about my baby being there." He'd said before he knew it.

Cashmere's eyes lit up. Hearing that made her so happy inside. He had never fully claimed the baby, but now he was. Or at least, he'd made an indication that it was.

"Anyway," he said feeling ready to move on to a more serious moment. "I have been thinking a lot and I would love to be a good father to my child. So, here's my proposal."

"Proposal? You make this thing sound so official like with legal documents I'll need to sign and shit."

"Well, it's not that serious, but I need to be clear that we're on the same page."

"Okay, I'm listening."

"If you need anything, I don't care what it is, I'll be here for you. I'll go to every single doctor's appointment if you want me to. I'll make sure to give you money weekly for whatever you may be craving, wanting, or needing. I want to make this pregnancy as easy for you as I can. I don't want you working or trying to work. I know how you feel about Shyla and in being there for her, but that's not a place for a pregnant woman to be working at. Not in my eyes, especially a woman that's pregnant with my seed."

"Okay," Cashmere softly eased in. "I'll talk to Shyla and let her know."

"Please do," Jabari told her. "I'm not trying to run your life, because I don't want you trying to run mine. So, I guess if you're interested in somebody that I'd have to accept that. However, I would rather you wait until you had the baby."

"Okaaaay," Cashmere reluctantly dragged. "I'm not interested in dealing with nobody at the moment. I just want to focus on my pregnancy and having a healthy baby."

"Good," Jabari told her.

"Buuuuuuttt, If I get horny—"

"Call ya boy. I got you."

Cashmere grinned. "I'm gon' hold you to that."

"You better." He told her with a handsome smile spread across his face. He laid back on the pillow just relaxing his head, as Cashmere ate a few crackers.

"So, how are you? I know it was hard racing tonight without Slick being there."

"Yea, it was hard as hell, but I know he was watching me from above."

"I'm sure he wouldn't have missed it for the world." She told him. "Have you been getting your rest lately?"

"Not really, but I'm good. I'm sure things will eventually go back to the way they used to be. The only difference is that he won't be around in the flesh."

"But, he'll be around." Cashmere assured him.

"You're right," he responded.

Cashmere then eased out of bed to use the bathroom. "That's another thing, I have to pee every thirty minutes it seems."

Jabari grinned with a shake of the head. "Damn, you just got it bad."

"Tell me about it," she said, as she headed into the bathroom smiling from ear to ear. It was nice to have Jabari there, and to top it off he called her instead of the other way around. He had started paying attention and she couldn't be happier. Accepting his proposal was nothing but a thing to her, because she needed a way in anyway. He made that part easy. Now, all she had to do was act right and eventually she'll get him back. After peeing, she washed up and then headed out of the bathroom. She smiled while shaking her head, as Jabari lay in bed knocked out.

"Dang, that was fast, and I didn't even get no dick." She joked, walking over and crawling into bed. As she lay there watching him peacefully sleep, his cell phone began to ring. She looked down at it to see a number calling. For Jabari not to have it saved, it had to be a woman. Wanting badly to answer it, she stared hard in his face to make sure he was sleep. The phone rang 2 more times, as Cashmere took in a deep, nervous breath and then without hesitation, she answered his phone.

"Hello," she said in a soft tone.

"Oh, I'm sorry. I must have the wrong number."

"Who were you calling for?"

"I have the wrong number." The caller responded.

"Okay." Cashmere responded, and then hung up the phone. She nervously looked over at Jabari. He must've been too tired because he didn't move. Next thing Cashmere knows the phone started ringing again. "Shit," she whispered, but quickly answered it.

"Hello."

"Um," the caller said, but then got quiet for a few seconds. "Is Jabari available?"

"He's sleeping. I'm sorry, who is this? This is Cashmere." She said, in hopes of letting a bitch know that she was still in the picture.

"Oh, okay. Well, tell him Tiana called when he wakes up. Thanks Cashmere." Tiana said, and then she ended their call.

Cashmere sat there holding Jabari's cell phone. Quickly, she sat it back down on the bed. Thoughts of what she'd just done started to play in her head. Just in case, Tiana mentioned it to Jabari, she'd have to think of what to say. They never played answering the other's phone. So, for her to cross that line was already bad enough. But, as she sat there, she came up with a plan or rather what she'd say. She just hoped it was enough, so that Jabari wouldn't cuss her ass out or cut her ass back off.

Chapter Eleven

Shyla sat behind the desk inside of her office with thoughts of Rich on her mind. He was supposed to be on his way to her house, but at the rate he'd been lying she doubted it. She started flipping through the books, looking at the tabs, the overhead and what the club was bringing in every night. Rich was going to be happy to see how well the club had been doing under her managerial skills. She was actually proud of herself with feelings of someday running her own bar or club. If she could do a job with that much success at Rich's club, she could certainly do even better numbers at her own.

Her cell phone started to ring, as Shyla looked away from the books to check out her display screen. It was Rich calling. Quickly, she answered it.

"Hey handsome."

"Hey Love, what you doing?"

"I'm at the club getting set up and making sure that all my workers get here on time."

"Your workers, huh?" Rich teased.

"Yes, my workers since I'm in charge now." She boastfully responded.

Rich grinned. "That's right. Ain't nothing wrong with that."

"So, where are you?" she pondered.

"Um, I won't make it there until in the morning. I'm sorry Babe. The club here is jumping and it's always something going on. Just delayed my flight," he explained.

"Yea, it's always something." Shyla mumbled.

"Don't be upset. I promise to come in the morning. Also, it's something I wanted to talk with you about."

"What's that?"

"It can wait."

"Is it bad?" she asked.

"No, it's actually good." He told her.

You leaving your wife?" she asked, as it got quiet on the other end. "Babe, you good? I was only joking."

"Yea, and I heard you. I was lost in thought for a moment. Anyway," he said to move on from what Shyla was supposedly joking around about. "I'm not going to hold you up. You can get back to work. Love you."

"Okaaaaay, but just in case we don't talk no more tonight, have a safe trip in the morning. Love you too." She said, and with that they ended their call.

"Knock, knock," Cashmere called out, as she knocked lightly on the office door and then walked in.

"Wassup Bestie, come on in," Shyla said.

"Girl, it's packed out there already."

"You know how Thursday nights are. Ironically, it's the littest night of the week at this club."

"I know."

"I thought you were off tonight. Only working Saturday night this week."

"Well, I needed to talk with you about my work schedule."

"You're taking a leave of absence already?"

"Well, kind of." Cashmere responded.

"Damn, I was only joking."

"Well, I'm not." Cashmere said. "I guess I should've told you this when I woke up Monday morning, but I'd had a blissful night with Jabari, and I didn't wanna ruin it. From then till now, I just kept putting it off."

"Damn, you make this sound serious as hell."

"You know how I am. I'm very loyal to you. You're the only person that I feel genuinely loves me regardless of my flaws. So, anytime you need me, even if it's just to fill in around here, I'm gonna do it."

"Calm down Cash. It's not that serious. You're good." Shyla grinned. "I was expecting you to eventually quit; especially since Jabari is paying your bills. You did mention that to me on Monday, so I kind of figured that it wouldn't be long before you dipped. Not just because of that, but mainly because you're pregnant. Shit when I was pregnant, I was just like you. All I wanted to do was stay home and kick back. Rich made that part easy too. He always took care of me. Well, I've worked as well, but it's been here."

"You make good money here though. It's not like he's giving that to you just because he owns the place. You still earn your keep."

"I agree."

"It's like since y'all met he's been training you to take over. That's why you're so good at it."

"It does seem that way. I just never thought about it like that."

"What is Rich up to?" Cashmere pondered with a frown on his face.

"I don't know. You think he's going to move to the West Coast for good and just leave us here? Maybe that's why he wants me to run the clubs."

"That would mean that he's not planning on being in your life anymore, but he still wants to make sure that y'all are financially straight. Is that something you want? I always thought you wanted the kids, the marriage, and the white picket fence."

"I do and if Rich leaves me he won't be leaving me hanging, because I'm gonna have the kids, the marriage, and the white picket fence. It just won't be with his ass."

"Damn, for the first time ever, I can see you mean business."

"I do. That's why I'm working hard and saving my money. My house is my house, my car is my car. He might pay bills, but nothing is in his name."

"That's the one thing we have in common. My house is my house and my car is my car, too. Thank God for Jabari. He didn't want shit in his name, either. Maybe that was his way of making sure I was straight. But, if he ever fully moves on, I'll have to pay the rent and my other bills. My car is almost paid off, so I ain't worried about that. But, that's why I'm going back to school. I need to get my shit together. I have a baby that needs me."

"Aww, listen at you. You're growing up on me." Shyla teased.

"Hush bitch." Cashmere said, while giving Shyla the middle finger.

"I have a doctor's appointment next week. Jabari is going to go with me."

"Well, that's good. I said that he'll start to come around. Jabari is a man first, so I'll know he'll do right by his baby."

"Yea, he will." Cashmere said, but then quickly changed the subject as something else dawned on her. "You know Skylar's birthday celebration is a month away. You know that's a big event they have every year. Normally, I go as Jabari's girl, but this year, what if he brings somebody else? I don't even know if I wanna go. I'd be too embarrassed; especially with me being pregnant."

"Girl, I don't believe he'll invite nobody else." Shyla said.

"He is talking to somebody else though."

"Who, Lauren's sister?"

"Yea, I believe so. She called him Sunday night when he was to my house, but he had fallen asleep. I answered the phone."

Shyla frowned. "What phone? His phone?"

"Yea."

"Omg, what'd he say?"

"He didn't say nothing because apparently he don't know. I thought she would've said something to him about it, but he hasn't said nothing to me—"

"Which means that she ain't said nothing to him."

"Exactly!" Cashmere agreed. "Hell, I already was gonna tell him that his phone rang, and I accidently answered it thinking it was you calling me on my phone. Hell, we both carry iPhones, they do look alike."

"That is true, because I've started to answer Rich's before, but it would've been by mistake. You better be glad she didn't say nothing; especially with you already trying to get Jah back on your good side. What the hell are you thinking?"

"I don't know. I just want this bitch to know that she ain't got Jabari to herself."

Shyla shrugged. "Well, that was one way to do it." She laughed.

"Hush bitch," Cashmere laughed.

"By the way, Justin gave me his number at the track Sunday night."

"You didn't tell me that bitch."

"That's because I haven't called him yet."

"So, but you like him?" Cashmere pondered.

"Yea, I actually do like him. I just don't wanna start talking to him while I'm still dealing with Rich."

"Girl, you better get with the program. Rich ass is married."

"I know that." Shyla mumbled with a roll of the eyes.

"Then act like you know it."

"Anyway," Shyla said, to change the conversation. "I hired somebody already. Their first night is actually tonight. She should be coming in soon."

"Oh, Thank Goodness. Now I don't feel so bad."

"You shouldn't feel bad anyway. I know you got my back just like I got yours. I do appreciate you working for me when I asked."

"Always," Cashmere said with a smile.

"Well, are you going to stick around tonight for a little while? I'm sure I can find you something to do."

"Hell nawl," Cashmere responded, quickly standing to her feet. "You won't get me." She laughed, walking to the door to the leave.

"You so nasty." Shyla laughed.

"I know."

Once Cashmere opened the door, she disappeared like she'd never been there.

As Shyla started going back over her paperwork, another knock was heard at the door. "You changed your mind?" she called out.

"No, my plans aren't changing for nobody." The unfamiliar voice said, as she entered the office.

Shyla looked up, as her heart dropped, and her eyes widened from shock.

"Hi Shyla I'm Kym. Kym Vega."

"I know who you are." *Rich's wife*, she thought.

"I'm sure you do." Kym said, as she walked over and stood in front of the desk. Shyla didn't know what to do. Was Rich's wife showing up to shoot her and then leave. She definitely wasn't prepared for this visit.

"What can I do for you?" she asked.

"That's funny you should ask. Hm, what can you do for me besides fucking my husband behind my back?"

"Hold up—"

"No bitch, you hold up." Kym said as she pointed her finger in Shyla's direction. "For years, I've sat back knowing that some lil homewrecking bitch was fucking my husband. For YEARS," she said with emphasis. One lil homewrecker after another. Then in comes you. See, you're one of the bold ones. The one that thinks she smart enough to have babies, so she's taken care of for the rest of her life. Well, I hate to burst your bubble. The nigga has a lot of kids."

"Nawl, wait a minute. Don't come in here acting like you know me—"

"I do know you. I know everything about you. I know where you live, what you drive, what time you shit in the mornings. I know you." She assured her with menacing eyes.

Shyla stood up behind the desk. "Bitch you been watching me?"

"No, I was watching him. You just happen to be one of the whores that was with him."

"Wow, so are we going to have an adult conversation, since you here? Or, do you plan on talking to me like I'm just some lil bitch that's gonna keep letting you?"

"Well—"

"Aht, Aht, hold on, because if that's what you think, you're sadly mistaken." Shyla told her with a mean stare.

"Okay, fine. Have it your way. It seems that's been happening a lot anyway," Kym said, as she glanced around the office space. "He's really putting you in position. I must say, he's never done that before."

"Putting me in position? Everything I'm doing I've earned."

"On your back?"

Shyla frowned. "Look lady—"

"Save the dramatics," Kym cut in. "You're not the only one."

"What?"

"I said you're not the only one. Unfortunately, you don't know the half, or you wouldn't be around. Not if you're as smart as I figured you to be."

"I'm so lost right now."

"I'm leaving Rich." Kym confessed. "Well, correction... I've left Rich. I moved back home about six months ago."

"Oh really?" Shyla uttered with an unsure expression.

"Not only was Rich fucking you, but he's been fucking another woman too."

"What now?"

"Ironically, this woman was in the picture before you. However, she just had a baby by him about four months ago."

"That can't be true."

"Oh, it's true." Kym told her. "Ask him, he won't be able to do nothing but tell the truth."

Shyla's heart was broken. All this time she thought that if Rich ever left his wife he'd be with her. However, she'd just found out that not only was there somebody else in the picture, but that she'd just given birth to his baby.

"You gotta be kidding me?"

Kym shook her head. "Oh, poor dear. You really thought you were the only one?"

"It's not about that."

"Of course, it is." Kym told her. "You had 2 boys by him, and you thought they would be the last of his heirs. Well, I hate to break it to you, they're not. Rich has always been a dog and it took me seventeen years of marriage to finally leave his ass. He's never going to be with just one woman and if you're cool with that then all you'll ever be is just another one of his women."

Shyla stood behind the desk, still not knowing what to say. Was Kym lying to her? She glanced down at her hand and true enough, there was no wedding ring there. From the serious look on her face it seemed like she was telling the truth.

Shyla cleared her throat, trying to find the right words even though there was nothing right about what really wanted to come out of her mouth. "So, you came in here to tell me that Rich is fucking another woman and that they just had a baby a few months ago? Not only that, but you left him 6 months ago?"

"Yes."

"Why would you want me to know this?"

"Why not?" Kym said. "I plan on taking Rich for everything he has. His plans are to put his clubs in your name that way I can't come after any of that money. But, he's planning on getting you to put them back in his name once this ugly divorce is over. That's why you're running his business for him now. He's basically preparing you for what's to come."

"Oh really?"

"Yes really."

"How do you know this?"

"How do I know this? Because his lawyer is fucking my lawyer and she put me on game. Yea, everybody is doing something shady these days to get what they want."

"I see," Shyla mumbled.

"So, is there another club on the West Coast?"

"What club? Rich has only been out there to beg me back. He doesn't stay long, only like a night or two to get in some time with the kids. Then he's right back on this end. When he's here he's either with you or the other bitch. Trust me, he's hardly on the West Coast."

"Wow!" Shyla said.

"I take it, he's not been with you."

"I think this conversation is over." Shyla said, as she walked over to the door to escort Kym out.

"Be careful. Rich isn't the man you think he is."

"You're just mad about something that you think you know. I'll make my own mind up as to what to believe after I speak with Rich."

"Don't shoot the messenger, even though it was plenty times I could've knocked you off."

"Wow, you threatening me?"

"No, I'm just saying." Kym said. "Oh, I don't know if he's gotten a storage or not, but if he gives you any furniture, it came out of my house."

Shyla scowled. "What?"

"Just know that Rich ain't doing nothing from the heart. He's trying to protect his assets and his investments." Kym explained. "The only thing I want from Rich at this point, is everything. I'm sure I may not succeed in getting it all, but I be damn if I'm not going to try."

By: Tiece

"So, I guess you're saying fuck me and my kids?"

"I never said that. However, I'm not fighting for your kids. I'm fighting for mine. On top of that, I had a ring on my finger. You don't." She said, as she headed out the door, but then stopped. "The other bitch I couldn't talk to like this. We've already fought a couple of times before you even came in the picture. If you think I'm disrespectful wait till you meet her. I wish you luck with that."

Shyla slammed the door shut once Kym was on the other side. So many thoughts plagued her mind. It felt like the room was spinning out of control, as she pressed her back against the door. Rich had definitely been lying to her. Sadly, she knew something was off. She just speculated the wrong thing. At that moment, she couldn't wait to talk to him. "LYING SON OF A BITCH!"

Chapter Twelve

"Mars, it's over. I don't know how many times I gotta tell you that." Skylar said, as she entered the house and then headed straight into the kitchen.

"But Skylar, please talk to me." Mars begged. "I need to know what's going on."

"I'm in love with someone else."

"Yea right, you're tripping right now."

"No, I'm being honest." Skylar told him.

"Come on. Just meet me at the spot."

"I'm not meeting you there no more. That spot is no longer our spot. You should never be there either. That's my family's property, so you know if they ever catch you out there they'll kill you."

"I know that. I ain't crazy." Mars told her. "But still, you can't meet me out there now? We need to talk. I love you."

Skylar rolled her eyes. "We are talking."

"Whatever I did, give me another chance. You're the only person that understands me."

"Mars, you're making this much harder than it should be. Just move on already."

"You're just going to disregard the time we spent together?"

"I'm not disregarding it, but I don't wanna carry on when I know it's over."

"Okay, Skylar."

Skylar stood in the front of the refrigerator looking for something. "Okay, I'll meet you later. I probably need to further explain what's going on. Maybe I do owe you that." She said while grabbing a bottle of water.

"Thank you," he said, and with that Skylar ended their call.

"Skylar!" Justin called out, as he startled her.

"Boy! You almost made me drop this." She said, with a nervous expression. "How long you been in here?"

"Not long," Justin responded. "But what was that call about?"

"What you mean?" she asked, knowing that she'd had Mars on speakerphone the entire time.

"I mean, I didn't know you and Mars had broken up." He responded.

"Well, um. That's none of your business." She told him.

"Maybe not, but I thought y'all were good. You've been acting all in love. Always out and about with him. Hell, he's the reason why Mom and Pops stay on yo' ass. They think he's a bad influence, but you don't. So, what's going on?"

Skylar shrugged, as she tried to walk off. Justin followed right behind her.

"How long have y'all been dating?"

Skylar shrugged.

"You know." He said.

"For about 2 years." She answered with an attitude.

"Okay, so for over 2 years we thought y'all were crazy in love."

"And, your point?" she asked, now heading up the stairs with Justin on her heels.

"My point is that I heard you say it was over."

"Okay and," she irritably uttered while entering her bedroom.

"Okay, so is it over?"

"Yea," she responded.

"You okay? I mean, what happened?"

"I talk to somebody else." She confessed.

Justin frowned. "How you just kick a nigga to the curb like that and is already talking to somebody else? You must've been talking to this new nigga."

Skylar sat on her bed. "No," she responded.

"Why you being so vague with me? We've always been tight and now suddenly you wanna keep secrets?"

"It's not like that." She said.

"Well, what's it like?" he pondered.

"Sit down," Skylar told him. "What I'm about to tell you is something you can never repeat. I don't care if it ever comes out, I don't need you saying nothing about this conversation. You got that?"

"Yea," Justin said.

Skylar shot him the side-eye. "You gotta promise me."

"Damn, it's that serious?" Justin asked.

"*I'm serious J or I'm not going to tell you if you can't promise like we've always done in the past.*"

"*Yea, but in the past those were just talks we'd have that never went any further. Like the time you stole 200 dollars out of Mom's purse to go to a party. Or, like the time you took 3 ounces of dope and gave it to Mars. Or, the time you took Cain's car while he was passed out drunk and stayed out all night, but was able to sneak back in before he woke up. Or, the time you told me you rubbed cocaine on your gums at the age of 14—*"

"*Okay damn!*" Skylar cut in. "*I've not been the picture-perfect frame of a good girl, never claimed to be. And for the record, I never fucked with coke again. The shit tasted nasty and had me feeling fucked up. That's a feeling for somebody else, not for Skylar.*" She retorted.

"*Good,*" Justin said. "*So, what's up?*"

"*You gotta promise J.*"

Justin shook his head. "*You can't be serious.*"

"*I'm serious.*"

"*Okaaaaay, I promise.*" Justin agreed.

"*I'm pregnant.*"

Justin nearly jumped off the bed. "*YOU'RE WHAT?!*" he asked in a screeching whisper.

"*Calm down.*"

"*Pops is going to kill you.*"

"*So, what. I'll be 19 years old tomorrow. I don't need nobody's permission to have a baby.*"

"*Yea, but you're breaking up with Mars. So—*"

"*Don't start giving me the third degree. That's all you need to know right now.*"

"*I need to know more,*" he insisted with a serious stare.

"*Well, if I tell you something please don't say nothing to nobody. I will tell them eventually, but I don't want you to.*"

"*I won't,*" he assured her.

"*I've been seeing someone new.*"

"*You've already said that. Who? Do I know him? How new is this person in your life?*" and just as she was about to say something…

"*What y'all in here talking about?*" Jabari pondered, as he entered the bedroom.

Skylar immediately stood up. "*We'll talk about this later.*" She told Justin. "*Hey Bruh,*" she said to Jabari, as he pecked her on the cheek.

"*Wassup Sis. Where you headed?*"

By: Tiece

"I got things to do. Ya girl is turning 19 tomorrow!" she cheered. "Y'all need to get out of my room, so I can shower and get ready for tonight."

Jabari laughed, as he looked over at Justin. "Is she okay?" he teased but was kind of serious.

Justin shrugged, "Yea, I guess." He responded after getting the side-eye from Skylar.

"Okay, bye y'all." She said, and then closed the door shut behind them.

Justin flinched out of his thoughts, as the loud chirping sounds of his cell phone going off startled him. He reached over on his bed next to him and picked it up. He checked out he display screen to see that it was a message from Shyla.

"Oh shit," he whispered, while opening the message to read it.

Hey Justin. I was laying here and thought about you. Hope all is well. SHYLA

"She thought about me?" he asked himself with a smile. He'd been waiting for this message for a week. There was no way he was passing up this opportunity.

Can I call you? JUSTIN

That's cool. SHYLA

He wasted no time calling her back. On the first ring she answered.

"Hello," she said in the sexiest voice ever.

"Hey Beautiful."

"Hey," Shyla spoke again.

Justin could see her smiling through the phone. "I've been waiting for this moment."

"Oh yea?"

"Yea," he responded with a smile. "How have you been?"

"I've been okay, can't complain." She responded. "What about you?"

"I'm good, always blessed." He answered.

"I thought you would've been in church on this good ol' Sunday morning. I was even wondering if you'd respond."

"Shit, I would've asked God to forgive me and messaged you back."

Shyla was tickled.

"Then I would've held up my finger and exited the church to call you. Hell, I would've even left church early for some of this conversation. He would've understood." He added, as Shyla laughed out loud.

"Well, our God is a forgiving God," she grinned.

"Amen," Justin agreed. "I've seen you around a few times and even asked about you way before giving you my number."

"When was that? Don't tell me it was the day you had to carry me to the car." She grinned. "That shit was so fucking embarrassing afterwards."

Justin laughed. "I bet it was, but nah it was before that. I saw you in the club a few years back and asked about you. I heard you were in a relationship or that you'd not long ago had a baby by him or something. So, I didn't press up on you."

"I wish you would've," Shyla thought, as negative thoughts about Rich surfaced.

"I started to shoot my shot." He joked. "But, anyway, back to you. I didn't know you was 'bout that gangsta life."

"Stop it, I'm already shame enough." She laughed out loud.

"No, but I'm serious. I thought my Pops was gonna have to call the police on y'all." He joked.

"Justiiiin! Your dad wasn't even out there?" she laughed.

"I know," Justin teased. "But aye, I liked that. You wasn't letting nobody jump on your cousin, whether she was right or wrong."

"Right, because I definitely thought she was wrong for that," she uttered.

"But ain't nothing wrong with having her back. I ain't gon' lie. That shit turned me on."

"Really?" she asked.

He could feel her smiling again. "For real. Me and siblings are the same way. Till this day we don't play that. Can't nan nigga run up and think the other 2 ain't coming along for the ride. He better come equipped, that's for sure." He told her.

"I feel you, because me and Cash have always had each other's back. She grew up a little harder than I did, and for that we built a solid bond that's unbreakable. I don't always agree with her choices, but I love her the same. She's like a sister, my best friend, and my 1st cousin all rolled in one."

"That's wassup." Justin eased in.

"My life isn't perfect either, but she never judges me. So, who am I her to judge her?"

"I wholeheartedly agree. I've never been that way, either. What you do is your business, the only way I involve myself is if you make it mine too."

"I feel you." Shyla said, while putting her hand inside of her panties and softly rubbing across her bare bottom. It was smooth to the touch, and just talking to Justin had her wanting to do some naughty things.

By: Tiece

"So, but what you doing besides laying there?"

"Oh, nothing. Just laying here," she responded, but wasn't exactly just laying there. She dipped her fingers inside of her lady pond, while relaxing to the soothing sounds of Justin's deep, sexy voice.

"Maybe I should've been laying there too."

"Maybe," she smiled.

"A'ight now." He told her, now grabbing his dick through his boxer shorts. Something about her voice had changed, becoming sweeter and more attractive. "I wanna see you soon for lunch, dinner, breakfast... Maybe all three," he slid in.

Shyla grinned, while grinding on her fingertips. "I'd love that." She softly responded. "Where would we go?"

With his head rested back on the pillow, he closed his eyes with seductive thoughts of her riding him. "Somewhere you've never been." He answered, while massaging his manhood back and forth.

Shyla grinned, with a whispered moan. "How do you know I've never been there?" she asked, as she gently rubbed her clit.

"Trust me, you've never been to this place before." He answered, as thoughts of hitting her from back took over the call. He imagined her bent over in the shower. One foot was propped on the shower seat, the other foot on the floor, as he caressed her wet walls from the back. Gripping her by the waist while planting his feet firmly to the wet floor, he stroked her creamy insides. Her juicy goods felt like warm butter embracing his dick. "Damn," he whispered.

"You alright over there?" Shyla asked, as she continued to dip in and out of her juice box.

"Yea, never better," he responded. Thoughts of them fucking from the shower to the bed now had his mind engulfed. With her legs spread apart and in the air, he watched his slithering python sliding in out of her slick tunnel. The look on her beautiful face and the curl of her toes had him in a daze. Pumping venom in and out of her, going deeper and deeper, as the sounds of Shyla's voice enticed him more.

"So, when will you be ready?" she softly asked.

"All I need to know is the time and day. I'll be there," he said, while holding his chopper in his hand, the urge of an erotic explosion had his heart beating faster and faster, and just as it started to bust, she said.

"I'm cummin'," she softly moaned.

Huh? Justin thought, as his eyes rolled back in his head.

"Um, damn." She mumbled. "Go watch TV, I'm coming." She called out. "Sorry, my boys were knocking on my door." She said, but was lying because her boys weren't home.

Justin got out of bed. "Oh okay, it's cool," he said while heading into the bathroom. "You good?"

"Yea, I'm good." She answered, as she made her way into the bathroom.

Both turned on their showers. "Well, I'm about to get my day started. It was really good talking to you. I hope this is just the start."

"You're taking me some place I've never been right?"

"Damn right. I'm glad you remembered that part." He said, as he stepped in the shower.

"How could I forget?" Shyla responded.

"Well, just like I waited for you to text, I'll wait for you to call me and set this date up."

"I'll make sure I do that and sooner than later," she assured him.

"I like the sound of that," he said.

"Cool." She responded.

"Cool," he said back with a smile on his face, and then they ended their call. He reached out of the shower to sit his phone down. With his eyes closed, he relaxed under the beating hot water cascading down his chocolate skin. As thoughts of Shyla danced around in his head, his eyes popped open like reality had just sunk in. "What the hell just happened?"

Shyla stepped out of the shower and ran right into Rich. "What the fuck are you doing here? You ain't been answering your phone since I talked to you Thursday night. Don't come running here now."

"I ain't running nowhere. I just knew you were pissed off, so I was giving you time to cool off."

"Cool off? Cool off, nigga?! How 'bout moved on."

Rich frowned. "What's that supposed to mean?" he asked, as he followed her into the bedroom.

Shyla started rummaging through her drawers, as she pulled out a pair of Victoria's Secret white panties and slid them on. "It means what the fuck I said." She told him, while putting on the matching bra.

"Shyla don't play with me."

By: Tiece

"It seems like you're the only one playing." She said as she slipped on a one-piece romper and then stood in the mirror trying to figure out what she was going to do with her hair. "So, how long has your marriage been over? Was that information you were ever going to share with me?"

"Babe, I wanted to, but—"

"But you didn't because you got another bitch that's riding too? Is that why you didn't tell me your wife had left you? Orrrrr, was it because you have a baby by your other side bitch?"

"See, that's why I didn't talk to you."

"No, you didn't talk to me because you're a pussy. I've sat here all this time, over the years thinking that you loved me."

"I do." Rich said while sitting on the edge of the bed.

"You don't love me. You only love yourself. You've been running back and forth to California, so you say. Yet, your wife shows up at the club and tells me that you're playing house with some other bitch that lives here. What the fuck Richard?"

"I'm sorry Babe. It's not what it looks like."

"Hell, I ain't seen it yet to even know what it looks like. Yo' dumb ass! So, are you fucking somebody that's been in your life before me?"

"Yea, but it didn't quite happen like that. She was before you, but then we stopped talking some before you and I started seeing each other. Then, she came back in the picture about a year ago. I'm sorry. I tried to stay away."

"Tried?! Tried?! So, you acting like you in love with this bitch if you TRIED, but still couldn't stay away!"

"I am," he confessed.

Shyla scowled. "You are what?" she pondered, like he better say the right shit or else.

"I am in love with her."

"Muthafucka!" Shyla screamed out, as she smacked him as hard as she could across his face.

"Hold up Shy!" he yelled out, reaching for her hands.

"No, don't touch me!" Shyla shouted. "You lying son of a bitch!"

"But, I love you too." He admitted. "I can't help it. I love all y'all."

"All of us?! Who the fuck is all of us?"

"You, her, and my wife." He confessed, with the sincerest look on his face, but was slapped again the minute those words left his mouth.

"You a nasty bitch! You can't possibly love 3 women." She said, still trying to fight him. Somehow, Rich was able to keep her at bay while blocking her licks. Eventually, she grew tired and calmed down just enough to keep her hands to herself.

"I wish I had been honest with you, but I knew you wouldn't like it."

"Damn right," Shyla told him.

"I never meant to hurt you. I never meant to hurt Kym—"

Shyla cut in. "And I guess you never meant to hurt her either, right?"

"Shy calm down."

"Don't tell me to fucking calm down!" she yelled. "Right now, I just want you out of here."

"Don't act like that. I really wanted to talk with you about putting the clubs in your name."

Shyla's eyes widened. "Oh really? And, why would you want to do this right now?"

"Honestly, I trust you. I know you're not my biggest fan right now, but I still believe in you. I believe in us." He told her. "Just do this for me and I promise you'll never have to work hard ever again. I'll always take care of you and our boys."

"So, you think that this is all it's about?"

Rich shrugged.

"You can't buy us Rich!"

"I'm not trying to. I just wanna be able to do right by y'all, but if you don't let me put the clubs in your name then I'm afraid that things will get ugly."

"And whose fault is that?"

"I don't have time for this Shy. My back is against the wall and I need you."

"What about her? Your other bitch? Why you ain't putting the shit in her name? That's who you're with the most."

"Please Shy. Let's not go back and forth about this. I don't trust her like I trust you."

"But you love her like you love me." Shyla told him, with a slick roll of the eyes.

"It's not the same." He said.

"Rich, I need you to leave right now!"

Rich got up off the bed and headed for the room door. "I'm giving you 3 weeks to decide what you're going to do. The sooner the better. Or—"

"Or what?"

By: Tiece

"Or, I don't know what I'm gonna do." He told her.

"Sounds like a personal problem to me," Shyla uttered. Just as Rich reached the door to walk out of her room, she asked, "Did that furniture come out of your house?"

Rich stopped in his tracks, as he turned to face her. "Yea," he responded, and then left just as quickly as he came.

"Wow." Shyla let out, as tears started rolling down her face. She went straight for her cell phone and then called Cashmere.

"Wassup Bestie?" Cashmere answered.

"What you doing?" Shyla asked.

"Trying to eat a burger. I'm excited about my appointment tomorrow. Mostly because Jabari is going."

"I know. Is he staying the night there?"

"I don't know, but what's wrong with you? You sound like you're crying."

"Rich came by."

"With his pussy ass, what he said?" Cashmere pondered with a scowl on her face.

"Let's just say that the furniture came out of his house."

"Bullshit!" Cashmere let out.

"No lie and that ain't all this woman said that was true."

"Damn Shy. I'll be over in a little bit."

"Thanks," Shyla said, as she ended the call.

Chapter Thirteen

Later that evening, Jabari sat on the leather sectional in front of his TV watching Harlem Nights. It was a movie that always lifted his spirits when he was down. He hadn't been out the house all day and with no food in his refrigerator, he was hungry as hell. His head had been all over the place. One minute he fine, the next he wasn't. Not only was Slick's death playing heavily on his mind, but also Skylar's. Things weren't adding up, but something told him that the two were related somehow. He replayed his last talk with Slick. It was a lot that was said, but only a couple of main things that stood out. One being that whatever he was following up hit close to home. Loosing Skylar was also something that hit close to home.

He rested his head back and closed his eyes, took in a deep breath and then let it out. His mind began to revisit the last conversation he'd had with his sister.

"Where you going?" Jabari asked.

Skylar turned to face her brother with an angry expression on her face. "To see if my spare key is in the lock box under my car." She said, while walking out the front door. Jabari got up off the couch and followed her.

"Aye, hey slow down." He called out, as Skylar turned to face him. She'd been crying and was clearly upset. "What is wrong with you?"

"I'm leaving this place and I'm never coming back."

"Quit talking like that." he worriedly told her. "Calm down," he said, as she started back walking towards her car. "Hey, stop and talk to me."

"Bruh, I'm just over this. If I could tell y'all what was really going on I would, but I know if I do Pops is going to be extremely pissed. He'll run and tell Unc and then all hell might break loose."

"Does this have something to do with what you told Justin?"

Skylar frowned. "Really? Did he tell you something?'

"No, he didn't tell me shit. But, I'm asking you. Be straight up with me. You know I've always had your back. Don't run from whatever is going on." He told her. "I see a suitcase in your backseat. What's that for? Sis, what are you doing?"

"I'm planning on leaving town."

By: Tiece

"You what?!"

"Shhh, hush. You talking to damn loud." Skylar told him.

"Wow, are you fucking serious right now? You ain't taking yo' ass nowhere."

"You ain't my father!"

"But I'm your brother and I love you too much to just stand by and watch you move away from us. What the hell, Sky. Like for real?!"

"Yes, I'm for real. That's the only way I'll be happy and not have to deal with y'all controlling asses." She told him while feeling under her car to see if her car key was in the lock box.

Jabari stood back, trying to gather his thoughts. The last thing he wanted was for his sister to move away and leave them behind. It would tear their family a part. It was bad enough that she'd just disappear whenever she felt like it, but at least she wasn't far. However, if she moved away they probably would never see her again.

"Sky, turn around and listen to me." He told her.

"B, I don't have time." She said, as she stood up and shook her head. "Damn, my key ain't in there."

"Why do you need your key so bad?"

"Because I'm meeting Mars later."

"What's going on with you and Mars?" he pondered while looking her over. Her skin was glowing, as her big, bright eyes stared anxiously at him. He stared at her.

"What? Why you looking at me like that?"

"I see what's going on here."

"What?" she asked, while putting one hand on her hip.

"You're pregnant."

"What?"

"That's right. You're pregnant." He told her.

"You don't know what you're talking about."

"Yes, I do, and that's why you wanna move. I've thought about it over and over again and that's it. That's the reason why you wanna get away so bad."

Skylar shook her head, as if to say that Jabari was wrong.

"Sis, you don't have to move because you're pregnant. Mom and Pops might be upset, but it won't be the end of the world. And you know that they'll accept this baby with open arms. You're grown, what can anybody say?"

"Yea, but they already say enough."

"Well, stand your ground. You have a birthday tomorrow. Tell 'em then. Let 'em know that you're pregnant. I'll even tell them that I support you. I'm sure if Cain and Justin knew they'd support you," he said, while thinking about Justin. "Justin knows don't he?"

Skylar nodded her head. "Yea, I just told him today."

"That's what he wouldn't tell me, but I knew it was something going on."

"He wasn't supposed to." Skylar said.

"I know y'all tight as thieves." Jabari teased, causing Skylar to laugh a little.

"See, it's not that bad. You don't have to make a hasty decision off of temporary feelings. Mom and Pops will understand. Trust me on this. I'm sure everyone will love you adding a new edition to the family. I'm happy. Like you just don't know, I'm really happy. Now, Mom and Pops won't have no choice but to let you live, be grown—"

"And great." She added.

"And great," he repeated, as he wrapped his arms around her.

"You really think they'll be okay with this?" she pondered.

"I know they will be. They love you and they'll accept whatever you have going on. You see they had no choice but to accept Mars. I'm still shocked every time I see him over here chilling."

"Yea, they did let up a lot once they knew who I was dating."

"That's all it is with them. They just wanna know what you're doing, what you have going on. I think if you talked with them more about that stuff instead of feeling like you gotta keep everything a secret, you'll be alright."

"You might be right."

"I am right." Jabari told her. "Look at you, all pregnant and shit." He grinned. "Mom will definitely be happy about this, and you know whatever she accepts, Pops will accept. He's like the Incredible Hulk to people that don't know him, but he's a big softie to us. You just gotta know how to finesse them. You used to be so good at it. What happened? You losing your touch, Sis?"

"Stop it," Skylar laughed.

"No, but I'm serious. You just started getting in your feelings and instead of using your skills to get what you want, you turned rebellious. This pregnancy can work in your favor. We both know it can, you just gotta trust me. You can't move." He said.

"Well, I guess you're right."

"Damn right I'm right. You don't wanna leave us at a time when you'll need us the most."

"You're right." Skylar told him.

"Skylar, me and your mom wanna talk with you." Biggs said while standing in the front door.

By: Tiece

"There goes The Incredible Hulk." Skylar uttered.

"Yea, but he's really just a softie to us. Remember that," Jabari told her.

"Promise you won't say nothing until I do."

"I promise, as long as you don't skip out on us."

"I promise." She said, as she gave him a hug. "I love you, Bruh."

"Love you too, Sis." Jabari said, as Skylar walked off to speak with their parents. Little did he know that would be the last time he would talk to her.

He took in a deep breath, while wiping the tears from his eyes. Just the thought of it all broke his heart into a million pieces. He was missing a lot in his life and the majority of it was 2 of the closest people in the world to him. That alone was a hard pill to swallow. As he sat up, trying to shake his thoughts, a knock tapped lightly on his door. He stood up, wiped his face again and headed to open it. He already knew who it was. The minute the door opened, he smiled.

"Where you going with all them bags? You got more?" he asked, taking the grocery bags out of Tiana's hands.

"No, this is it." She responded, as she walked in the house behind him. "I thought you were just bringing me some of what you cooked today. I didn't know you were bringing groceries too."

"Well, I just wanted to make sure you were good, since you told me that your refrigerator was empty."

"It is." He grinned.

"I still bought you some of what I cooked today." She said, reaching in one of the bags and pulling out a Tupperware bowl with the sections in it.

"Thank you, cause I'm starving." He told her, and then wasted no time pulling off the lid. "Damn, it's still warm."

"Yea, I heated it before I left the house." She told him. "I remember you saying you hadn't gotten a microwave yet."

Jabari smiled while looking down at the food. Tiana had cooked macaroni and cheese, fried party wings, corn on a cobb and homemade cornbread. He wasted no time digging in.

Tiana started removing the groceries from the bag. "You don't mind if I put this stuff up do you?"

"No, and I appreciate you looking out for me. Thank you," he said. "Come here. Give me some sugar for that."

Tiana leaned in to kiss him. "No problem," she said, while removing the milk from the bag and putting it in the refrigerator."

"Whoaaa, you got my Frosted Flakes and Cinnamon Toast Crunch. You been listening to a nigga."

"Of course, I have." Tiana smiled. She pulled out a pack of lunch meat and a loaf of bread and put that away. She pulled out a carton of eggs and some cookies and ice cream, and then put that away.

"Butter Pecan ice cream, you have been listening." He teased, but was very serious.

"I keep telling you I pay attention to detail."

"Yes, you do." He told her while watching her put the food away.

Tiana simply grinned. "You're funny." She told him. "So, how is the food?"

"The food is delicious," he said, while biting one of the chicken wings. "You do know how to cook. This mac and cheese taste like my mama's."

Tiana laughed. "You tripping."

"No, I'm for real." He assured her.

"I'm glad you made time for me tonight, because this week I'll be super busy working on my blog. I have a few short stories to write."

"Okay, that's wassup. I respect the hustle." He said. "I'm gonna check out your blog one day."

"I think you should." She encouraged him. "What do you have going on this week?"

"Well, tomorrow I'm going to a doctor's appointment that Cashmere has."

"Oh okay."

"I don't really know what else I'll be doing this week. I know I'll be at the shop working though. It's always something for us to do there."

"I bet," Tiana said, as she continued putting up packages. "So, how do you feel about the appointment tomorrow?"

"I'm pretty cool about it. I think it's too early to know what she's having, but I think it's important that I be there."

"I understand."

"There is a chance the baby is mine, probably a stronger chance than I want to believe. But, I wanna do what's right and that's take care of my responsibilities. Cashmere ain't my lady, she knows that. However, if she needs me I'll be there. No matter what that may include."

"I understand." Tiana said.

"I don't want you to feel no type of way about it, because I'm not with her. I'm technically not with anybody, but I'm feeling you. I don't mind what we have right now. Will it turn into something serious? I don't know, but I'm not rushing it because I want it to be right. Especially if it's meant to be," he told her. "Cashmere is young too, so be careful when it comes to her. Don't let her get under your skin and run you off. She can't help it, she's just petty like that. Maybe it's her age and in knowing that she still has a lot of growing up to do—"

"Or, she's just protective over what she loves. Hell, I can understand that too. As long as she keeps her distance, I'm good."

"That's all I can ask." Jabari said, with a smile. "I just wanna keep it real with you. I don't wanna have secrets that could potentially hurt you or undermine what we share."

"I appreciate your honesty and I'm glad that we're able to talk like this."

"Me too. Now, what's up with you and that jacket?"

"You don't like my jacket?" she asked, while turning to face him.

"Yea, I like them thick legs showing under it. Let's not forget about the stilettos. You wore those in the grocery store?"

Tiana giggled, "Yea why?"

"Damn, I'm surprised a nigga didn't follow yo' fine ass out here." He told her with a handsome smile.

"They weren't crazy."

"I'm glad they weren't, but I'm crazier." He told her.

She thought about him knocking Kory out on her porch. "And, I believe you." She laughed.

"Is it chilly outside?"

"It is, but it's about to get real warm in here." She told him while untying the knot that kept her knee-length jacket closed. The jacket fell to the floor, as she propped both hands on her hips.

"Daaaaaaamn, you got a nigga 'bout to drool at the mouth." Jabari clowned, but meant every word.

"You like it?" she asked, showcasing her lace melon blue bra and panty set with the matching thigh-highs strapped to a melon blue, adjustable garter.

"Wow," he said, eyes bright like a Kennedy 50 cent. "Damn," he pushed his food away.

"You ready for dessert?"

"Hell yea," he said.

Jabari walked over and picked Tiana up in the air. He walked her over to his kitchen table and sat her on it.

"People eat here." She teased.

"I'm people and I'm the only one that's about to eat here." He told her.

"Damn, you're naughty."

"And you look nice as hell in this lingerie."

Tiana smiled, as Jabari pulled her panties off. He softly licked her clit in circular strokes, getting her aroused and ready for what he had planned to go down. He placed his hands just so he could grip her hips while softly kissing her lips. She had become his desert and he was going to indulge for as long as she could take it. In no time, Tiana began to cum as she held his head, while trying to squirm out of his grip.

"Aht Aht, where you going?"

"Baaabe," she called out from pleasure.

"No, we're just getting started." Jabari said, as he lifted her off the table and carried her into the bedroom. He was about to lay it down and then put her to sleep, like Rock–a–bye Baby.

Cashmere wiped the clear gel off her stomach, as she got down off the examination table. She threw the paper towel in the garbage, while pulling her shirt back down and then sat in the empty chair by Jabari.

"So, what'd you think?"

"She has a strong heartbeat." Jabari responded with a smile.

"We didn't learn the sex yet, so why do you keep saying that the baby is a she?"

"I just know it." He said.

"I know what this is." Cashmere laughed. "You just want to say it's girl, in hopes that it'll be the opposite, a boy."

Jabari laughed. "Nah, I really want a girl."

"Yea, yea, if you say so." Cashmere teased, as Jabari's phone chirped of an incoming message.

He pulled it out his front jeans pocket, and then glanced down at the display screen. He opened the message, as Cashmere rolled her eyes like she knew who it was.

I know you're busy and I hope I didn't disturb you, but last night was amazing. I just couldn't help but hit you up to say that. TIANA

Jabari smiled on the inside, while keeping a straight face on the outside. He slipped his phone back in his pocket and looked over at Cashmere. "How did you feel about the sonogram? Was it everything you expected?"

Cashmere shrugged her shoulders. "I guess. I just can't wait until we find out the gender."

"Oh, so you're not having one of those gender-reveal parties these women be having?"

Cashmere laughed. "How do you know about those?"

"They're all down my IG timeline. Can't help but to know about 'em." He explained.

"I don't know. Do you want to?"

Jabari shrugged. "I'm down with whatever you wanna do."

"Well, some people have really nice ones. I might wanna have one. I'll think about it and let you know what I decide."

"Cool," Jabari said.

"Have you told your mama, yet?"

"Yea, I told her. My family knows and we're all just waiting patiently."

"Waiting patiently to see if it's yours?" she pondered.

"That too." Jabari coolly responded. He didn't want her to think that he wasn't going to have a blood test. He didn't care if the baby looked just like him, he wanted to make for sure. That would be the only way to put his negative thoughts to bed.

"Well, it is what it is." Cashmere uttered. "I'm glad your sisters party is next month. I'll be able to wear what I wanna. Hopefully, I'm still this size." She said.

"I don't even know what I'm wearing. Haven't really thought about it much, but I need to get myself in gear because a month goes by so fast. That party will be here before you know it."

"What's the theme this year?"

"At first we were going with a Masquerade Ball, but since it's somebody clearly hiding in plain sight, we decided that allowing masks would be prohibited. So, now we're going with a Hollywood Black & Bling themed event."

"Hollywood, like as in a celebrity type of event?"

"Yea, like a red-carpet event with pictures flashing, women dressed like royalty, men smelling like money. We're having a self-served buffet."

"What's on the menu?"

"Seafood." He told her.

"Oooooh, I can taste it now." Cashmere joked.

"Of course, we'll have other food choices for those that don't eat seafood. But, seafood is the main entrée."

"It's going to feel funny not going with you as your date. The first one I attended was the second y'all had. We started seeing each other a year after she passed away. You didn't invite me that first year." She clowned. "Must've had somebody else there."

Jabari grinned. "Nah, I just didn't feel it was time for us to come out yet. Not at my sister's first celebration. That time was for her absence to shine. I didn't want to be the talk of the party because I had somebody new on my arm."

Cashmere frowned. "I guess I understand." She uttered. "Well, so this year I won't be on your arm?"

"No, you already answered that earlier. However, since we're discussing this, I hope you don't mind that I invited Tiana."

"Oh really?" Cashmere pondered.

"Yea, I think it'll be a nice party for everybody. Why not invite her?"

Cashmere rolled her eyes. "I hear you."

"Coming in," Doctor Taylor said, as she entered the exam room. "Here is your prescription for your prenatal vitamins and something you can take for nausea. Do you have any questions for me?"

Cashmere shook her head. "No," she responded. "I'll see you back in 6 weeks. At that time, you'll be 14 weeks pregnant. We might even get to see the gender of the baby."

Jabari smiled. "It's a girl." He whispered.

"Whatever," Cashmere grinned. "We have no questions."

"Okay, well give this paperwork to the clerical associate and she'll give you a card with your next appointment date and time."

"Okay, thank you," Cashmere said, as she and Jabari stood up.

"Thanks," Jabari said.

"Y'all are welcome."

They followed the doctor out into the hallway. She went in one direction and they went in the other. As they stopped at the front desk, Cashmere handed over her paperwork and waited to get what she needed to leave.

A woman walked into the doctor's office and bumped right into Jabari, as he stood waiting by the door.

By: Tiece

"Jabari," she called out.

Jabari looked at her. "Tiny," he said. "What you doing here? I thought you had gone back after Slick's funeral."

"No, I actually decided to stay for a while. My family needs me here. Slick's death took a toll on us all." She told him.

"Tell me about it."

"Even though we were first cousins, he was more like a brother to me. He told me a lot shit."

"I know he did." Jabari said. "Y'all were pretty tight, even after you moved away."

"I know right," she said.

"So, what are you doing here? You pregnant?"

Tiny laughed. "Boy, get outta here. You see me with this uniform on. I work here." She informed him.

"Ooooh, okay." He said, just as Cashmere walked over. She looked at Tiny like a deer caught in headlights.

"Hey, Cashmere right?" Tiny pondered, with a slight frown on her face.

"Hey," Cashmere nervously spoke.

"I didn't know y'all were still a couple." Tiny said, before she knew it.

"I guess Slick told you that too." Jabari joked, but was very serious.

"Yea," Tiny grinned. "Oh wow, you're pregnant?"

"Yea," Cashmere nodded.

"How far along?" Tiny asked.

"Jabari I'm feeling queasy. I need to get out of here and get some fresh air," she said, like she didn't hear Tiny. Without answering her period, she opened the office doors and walked out. "Whew, I feel sick." She said like she was about to faint.

Tiny hugged Jabari. "You better go tend to that."

"I know right. That's all she do, eat and throw up." He clowned. "It's good to see you. I'm sure we'll see each other around. As a matter of fact, stop by my parent's house and get an invitation to Skylar's 7th year celebration next month."

Tiny smiled. "I'll be sure to do that. It's good to see you too." She said, and with that Jabari exited the office, leaving Tiny with a million and one questions traveling through her mind.

"What the hell did I just witness?" she pondered.

Chapter Fourteen

"I can't believe how much I've grown in a month. This some bullshit." Cashmere said, as she and Shyla pulled up to *The Brick House*, a building where lavish events were usually held.

"Yea, your ass is gonna be huge girl." Shyla grinned, while looking for a parking spot. "I hope we ain't gotta walk far. These heels I got on won't allow me."

Cashmere laughed. "Just put me out at the door Bitch."

"You one dirty muthafucka!" Shyla laughed.

"I'm serious Bitch." Cashmere nodded, just as Shyla found an up-close parking spot. "Thank ya Jesus!" she said, waving her hands in the air. "There is a God."

"I know that's right." Shyla chimed in.

"I'm excited and nervous at the same time."

"Me too," Shyla responded. "Justin invited me as his date tonight."

"Girrrrrl, I'm so happy for you. But, being that you drove me here, since I don't have a date," she uttered with a roll of the eyes and then continued. "How will that work? I mean, with you being his date."

"Well, when we get up to the doors I'll let someone know that I'm with him. They'll call him to come up front and escort me inside the party."

"Oh wow, bougie shit!" Cashmere clowned with a big smile spread across her face. "I love it. But, I can't believe Rich went for that shit."

"Fuck Rich."

"Damn, so do you really believe it's over with y'all?"

"I don't know. I still talk to him, because I did allow him to put those clubs in my name, but I told him I needed space."

"So, when the time comes for you to turn the clubs back over to him, will you?"

Shyla shrugged. "I don't know girl. Right now, I still get my managerial pay, but if that doesn't change he won't be getting shit back. Running the clubs ain't no joke. Now, his dumb ass done started showing back up—"

"But that's only because you found out about him lying. The nigga don't even have a club on the West Coast."

"Exactly!"

"It's so many lies he's told me over the years that I forget to address some of the stuff when we talk. Some of it doesn't hit me until we go our separate ways. I just can't with him. Once his wife snitched on his ass shit ain't been the same. Whoever this other woman is, he loves her and I believe more than me. From what I'm told was that she left him years ago because he wouldn't leave his wife. Now, the table has turned, and the wife has left him, but somehow he's back with the other woman. Nigga just left me out the equation like me or boys didn't exist."

"Well, he's still taking care of you financially."

"I'm taking care of my damn self. I do more shit at them clubs than he does." Shyla said.

Cashmere nodded her head to agree. "I feel you. I just never thought Rich had so much extracurricular shit going on. And daaaamn, he got a lot of kids."

Shyla laughed. "His dumb ass. Long as he makes sure me and mine are good, I'm good. Other than that, we can move past this subject just like I'm moving past his ass."

"Say less," Cashmere said. "I'm nervous. What if Tiny is here?"

"Who? Talking about Slick's cousin?"

"Yea," Cashmere responded.

Shyla gave Cashmere the side eye. "What's up with that? You being real vague when it comes to this Tiny chick, but you've brought her name up a few times."

"She knows about me and Slick."

Shyla's eyes widened. "Why you ain't been said that?"

"Well—"

"Well what?"

"Well, I haven't been exactly honest with you."

"Girl don't give me too much before I go in this party. Anything that's big I would think you would've been told me about it."

"But—"

"But nothing." Shyla said. "Look, just tell me tomorrow. I already got enough shit on my mind and to top it off, I'm anxious about tonight. I'm stepping out with someone new, that's big for me. I don't wanna add nothing you've done unsettling to it."

"Okay," Cashmere uttered.

Shyla frowned, before opening the car door. "Is that baby Jabari's?"

"Yes," Cashmere answered.

"How you know?"

"I just know it is. I can feel it. I know this his baby."

"Hm," Shyla mumbled. What she wanted to hear was that he'd been the only one Cashmere slept with, but since she didn't say that, it was no telling what she had going on. "Okay then, that's all I wanna know. We'll talk about the rest of this tomorrow."

"Fine."

"Girl, what you doing?" Tiana asked, as she looked over at Lauren.

"I'm sipping my drink before I walk off in this bitch."

"No, I'm talking about what did you just take?"

Lauren looked over at her sister and smiled. "I popped an ecstasy pill."

Tiana scowled. "You what? When you started popping pills and where did you get it from?"

"Cain has anything you could possibly want. Lately, I've just been exploring some of the good stuff."

"The good stuff? Yo' ass better not be doing this shit on a regular."

Lauren laughed. "Girl, I'm not. I've only taken a pill here or there. You know I don't fuck with none of that other shit." She assured her, while firing up the joint in her hand. "Just weed and a pill, every now and then," she said, toking from the joint.

"Okaaaay," Tiana dragged.

"I'm excited about this part, but it already feels different this year."

"What you mean by that?"

"First off, I rode here with you not my man."

"Bitch don't do me." Tiana cut in. "If you wanted to ride with your man you could've. I just didn't want to walk in by myself."

Lauren laughed. "Sis, you know I got you. It ain't about that. But Cain's kids are supposed to be here tonight too."

"To this event?"

"Yea, he invited both of his baby mama's just so his kids could be a part of this. I don't know if his daughter's mom will show up with her, but it'll be interesting if she does. I've never met that one. I've only seen her on social media. The other one is Hoe'ratchet." She made up.

Tiana grinned. "She doesn't really look it though, but I believe you. I was shocked how cute the baby was dressed with his lil Beats on his ears."

"Yea, he was cute."

"I know you said the first time you saw him he was dirty."

"He was, his face and all was dirty. But, I see she stepped up her A-game. She better had because I'm gonna talk about the bitch. I don't give a damn."

"No, you don't."

"You're good with this though." Tiana asked with a concerned stare. Lauren had never done anything other than weed, so to see her pop a pill was something new and different.

"Yea, I'm good. I'm just living my best life. I can't let these bitches get to me and I can't let 'em have my man. I know I was slacking in the sex department, but I realized I had to step my game up."

"Hm," Tiana mumbled. "Well, I can feel you on that part. But hey, keep your head up at all times and never lose focus on yourself. I don't want you to start doing stuff that could lead to you doing bigger stuff."

"Girl, not me. I know what I'm doing."

"Okay, I was just saying. I know it can be stressful dealing with something of this nature. That's why me and Derek didn't make it. He had a daughter by one of his side bitch's. I guess it's cool now because she and Ashley are only a few months apart in age and are really tight with each other."

"They should be, they look just alike. Hell, you would think that's your daughter too."

Tiana laughed. "Everybody says that."

"They're the only 2 Derek has right?"

"Yea, he ain't had no more yet. But you can't count his hoeish ass out."

Lauren laughed. "Yea, he is that. Guess he learned how to strap up, though."

"I would hope so."

"Back to Cain. I'm surprised he'd invite his kids to something like this."

"Well, the celebration is for their late aunt, his only sister. Plus, he told me that if the kids come they'll be leaving early before the real festivities begin. Like the loud music and dancing," she added.

"Oh okay."

"How do you feel with this being your first time attending this event?"

"I feel good. I'm surprised I never wanted to come in the past. I thought it was some sad occasion where y'all reflected on Skylar's life."

"We do reflect on her life, but it's definitely not meant to be a sad event. Skylar loved life. She was always the life of the party, so that's what these parties are about."

"I see, look at all these cars and people here."

"It's packed like this every year." Lauren said. "The food is always delicious and the crowd is always for the grown and sexy."

"Bitch, in all these years you never explained that it was this type of event."

"Bitch, yes I did. Yo' homebody ass just ain't never wanna go."

"Well, guess who's out the house now Bitch?"

Lauren laughed. "Been getting out a whole lot lately since you been kicking it with Jabari."

A smile spread across Tiana's face. "Yea, I really like him. He's really the Goat in more ways than one."

Lauren playfully shot her the side-eye. "Yea, I bet. I bet he's in there waiting on you," she said, just as Tiana's phone chirped of an incoming text message.

Hey Babe, where you at? JAH

"Speaking of the Angel."

Lauren laughed out loud. "Not the angel, it's supposed to be the devil."

"Nah, not in his case," Tiana laughed, while messaging him back.

I'm out here in the parking lot. We're about to come in shortly. TIANA

Okay, ask for me when you make it up to the door. I'll come escort you in. JAH

Awww, okay cool. TIANA

"He said to ask for him at the door and he'll escort me in."

"Well ain't that sweet of him." Lauren smiled.

"I told you he's the Goat."

"Yea, yea." Lauren teased. "I know one thing I feel so damn good. I ain't letting no baby mama drama get to me tonight. I'm going in this bitch and have me some fun."

"I know right. Me too," Tiana agreed. "You about ready to get out?"

"Hell yea, let me text my man and tell his ass to meet me at the door too." Lauren said, as she and Tiana got out of the car. The night was young, and they were definitely going to make the most of it.

"Husband, are you okay? The party is getting started and you're off ducked in the back all by yourself."

"I just have a lot on my mind." Biggs said.

"Honey, now is not the time to be thinking when you have a building full of people here celebrating our daughter's birthday." Karen said, as she walked over and rubbed him gently on the back.

"I know, it's just that this time of the year is always hard for me."

"I know dear, but you got to show your face. We're the reason this party is happening."

"Yea, but Skylar should be here. And I know you're going to say she is here, but no she's not. She's gone, dead and gone—"

"Samuel McCoy, please get it together."

"Somebody took my baby girl, my only daughter," he said, feeling choked up. "I haven't slept good since that happened."

"Me either, but we have to go on." Karen told him. "It's hard on me too. Probably even harder, but tonight I have to be strong for her even if I break down tomorrow. This is her night. We can't forget that."

"I know, but we missed out on so much when we lost her."

"I think about it every day." Karen agreed. "It's one of the hardest things that I've ever had to deal with. I get sick when I think about her smile and the joy she brought to this family, because she's no longer around. It's hard on me, on you, and the whole family."

"I know," Biggs said. "Slick's death is taking a toll on me too. I can't let that go because I don't know why he was killed in the first place. But, I feel like if I can't find out what really happened to Skylar then it'll lead me back to what happened to Slick."

"We all know Mars had something to do with Skylar and he's not around. He hasn't been around in 5 years. Maybe he's gone for good too. Who knows? Even if he was still alive and well he wouldn't come back this way."

"Well, you're right about that." Biggs uttered, already knowing that him and Papers made sure Mars would never come back.

"I have to get back out here. I know people are looking for us. Plus, we have a speech to make in about an hour. I need to have a few glasses of wine and unwind." Karen said.

"I do too, but what I need right now is just a little more time to get myself together and then I'll join the party. Matter of fact, can you round up Papers, Cain, Jabari, Justin and Bruno for me. Send 'em back here where I'm at. I really need to have a quick chat with them."

"Right now?"

"Yes, you can tell one to tell the other and so on. Don't worry, it won't take long. I promise I'll be out soon." He said, while leaning down to kiss her.

"Okay, I love you."

"I love you to," Biggs responded.

Karen smiled, but with worried eyes and then left the room. Biggs sat down in one of the empty chairs while in solitude. He was drained for some reason and really needed rest like yesterday, but how could he sleep with so much going on around him. It was one thing after another, didn't seem like his family was ever going to catch a break. He took in a deep breath while drinking his whiskey straight.

"So, what were you and Jabari talking about?" Biggs asked.

Skylar shrugged. "Nothing much," she told him.

"Me and your mom wanna talk with you."

"About what now?" she pondered with a sour expression on her face.

"It's nothing bad, Sky." Karen cut in. "We just don't want to lose you."

"What you mean, lose me?"

"I mean, we've paid attention you as of lately and you're hiding something. I haven't put my finger on it yet, but I just want you to know that you're grown."

"Yes, you're grown now," Biggs slid in. "I know me, and your mom have been hard on you over the years, but it was out of love. I've never intentionally meant to hurt you or make you feel less than—"

"Because you're everything to us." Karen cut in. "Our world wouldn't function right without you in it."

"Awww, what's this really about?" Skylar asked.

"It's about us giving you your freedom. It's about us not hounding your whereabouts. It's—
"

"*About us allowing you to make your own decisions from this point on. You'll be 19 as of 12a.m.—*"

"*A grown woman,*" Karen cut in. "*And from this point on we're going to treat you as one.*"

"*Wow, meaning I can stay out all night and y'all not aggravate me or ask me a million questions as to where I've been?*"

"*Yes, as in all of that.*" Karen told her. "*See, we just wanna make it right. We don't wanna keep going back and forth with you. We love you.*"

"*That's right, we love you,*" Biggs agreed. "*And, you know there is nothing in this world we wouldn't do for you.*"

"*I know.*" Skylar said. "*I love y'all too. Which is why I believe now is the time to tell y'all—*"

"*Tell us what?*" Karen asked with curious eyes.

"*Well, um.*"

"*Well,*" Biggs said, as he anxiously waited. With Skylar it was no telling what was going to come out of her mouth, so he knew he had to be prepared.

"*Um, well, Mom and Pops, I'm pregnant.*" She confessed.

Biggs and Karen's mouth dropped open. Both somewhat shocked.

"*You're what?*" Karen asked. "*Did I hear you right?*"

"*Yes ma'am.*" Skylar responded. "*I'm pregnant.*"

"*Oh wow,*" Biggs said, as he found himself sitting down to think first and then react later.

"*You okay Pops?*" Skylar asked. "*I had intentions of running away. I didn't know how to face y'all. I was actually leaving in the morning, but I don't wanna go.*" She admitted.

"*You're not leaving us. I'm glad that you decided to let us in.*" Karen told her. "*We truly appreciate that. Right Samuel?*"

Biggs cleared his throat, his eyes filled with water. This wasn't what he was expecting. His daughter was pregnant at 18 years old, and there was nothing he could do about it. He looked over at her. She looked confused and scared, which was the last thing he wanted her to feel. He wasn't happy about her news, but what could he do? The deed was already done.

"*Your mother is right Skylar.*" He finally said. He could see the relief as it covered her face. Her body language had changed in just that split second, as she smiled from ear to ear. He could tell that's all she ever needed was his blessing about anything she really cared about. "*I'm grateful that you came to me and your mother. I don't know what I would've done to know that you were out there somewhere and carrying our grandbaby.*"

"*That's the truth,*" Karen agreed. "*That's a scary thought. I'm actually happy about you expanding our family. Don't seem like the boys are trying to do it.*" She teased, as Skylar laughed a little. "*Now, this doesn't mean that you're not going to pursue your dreams. Your father and I will do everything we can to make sure that you go to college and graduate, so that you can build a solid foundation for your baby."*

"How does Mars feel about the baby?" Biggs asked.

"Well," Skylar said with a pause. She definitely didn't want to ruin the moment. "He's excited."

"He was actually going to allow you to leave without consulting with your family first?"

"Especially with him knowing you're pregnant. He should've known that wasn't a good idea."

"Actually, he's the one that told me I should stay and just tell y'all the truth."

Biggs eyebrows raised. "Oh really?" he pondered. "Okay, there may be hope yet." He uttered.

"Daaad."

Biggs shrugged. "I'm just saying, baby girl." He teased.

"You let him know that I would like to talk with him as soon as possible." Biggs told her. "We need to have a man to man conversation. He needs to be able to take care of his family."

"Well," Skylar cut in, but then decided not to say anything.

"You okay?" Karen asked.

"Yes ma'am." Skylar responded, as she rubbed her small protruding belly.

Karen still couldn't tell that she was pregnant. "Skylar how far along are you?"

"I'll be 7 months in 2 weeks.'

"You'll be what?!" Karen and Biggs nearly asked at the same.

Skylar nervously grinned. "I'm just not big, but the doctor assured me that the baby is fine. She's growing at a healthy pace. Her weight looks good." Skylar assured them.

"Her, as in it's a girl?" Biggs asked.

"Yes sir, it's a girl." She said with a slight smile on her face.

Biggs had gotten teary eyed before he knew it. "It's a girl. My baby girl is having a girl." He said, with joy in his tone. He stood to his feet and walked over to hug her. "We love you. Don't you ever doubt that, and we'll help you raise her for as long as you need us."

"I'll always need y'all." Skylar told him. "I love y'all too."

"So, we have a lot of planning to do. It's going to be last minute, but you are having a baby shower. I don't care what you say." Karen told her.

"I'd like that." Skylar agreed, causing Karen to smile from ear to ear. "Do y'all mind if I go see Mars for a little while? I need to let him know that I gave y'all the news and that we won't be moving."

By: Tiece

"Thank God," Biggs uttered. "Oh and tell him that we need to talk the minute he's available."

"I won't forget Dad." Skylar gave her mom a hug and kiss, and then hugged her father. "Thank you," she whispered in his ear and then kissed him softly on the cheek. "I'll be back tonight. I won't be staying out," she assured them. "Love y'all." She said, and with that, she exited the room. Little did they know that would be the last time they'd ever see her alive again.

Chapter Fifteen

"Bestie, they really did the damn thing this year." Cashmere said, as she sipped from her cranberry juice."

Shyla nodded her head to agree. "Yea, it's really pretty in here with all the lights, the red carpet, the enormous buffet—"

"And, don't forget all these people dressed like they're attending an after party at the Oscars. Makes me wanna go shopping."

"The whole crew is wearing tailored suits and every last one of 'em has a pair of Louboutin Red Bottoms on their feet. I must admit, you and Justin look so good dressed in the same baby blue colors. Y'all look sophisticated and bougie at the same damn time."

Shyla grinned. "We do look good together. I never realized how handsome he was."

"That's because you never looked at any man but Rich."

"With his disrespectful, stupid ass." Shyla uttered. "But, Justin look so good tonight I'm thinking about giving him some."

"I'm surprised you haven't did it yet."

"He's the one that don't wanna go there. He knows the situation with Rich and he ain't with the games. Period," she added. "So, he's been making sure that I'm completely over it before he takes it there."

"Well, he must really like you to do that. Most nigga's won't care if you're married, as long as you're giving up the goods that's all they want."

"Apparently, sex ain't all he wants."

"Do you want more, because it seems like it can go that way if y'all ever hook up?"

"Hell yea, I want more, and I'd love to have it with him." Shyla admitted.

"Aww, I like that." Cashmere said, just as she looked up to see Jabari and Tiana talking. "See, that's what I'm tripping about." She said with a frown on her face. "It's bad enough that he walked her in, but damn can he get out of her face already?"

"Chill out Bestie." Shyla told her. "This is definitely not the event to act a fool."

"I'm good. I'm just gonna sit back and play my cards right. I ain't giving her or him the time or day to take me out of character."

"Good," Shyla said, just as Justin walked back over.

"May I have this dance?" he asked Shyla. "You don't mind do you, Cashmere?"

"No, by all means sweep this pretty lady off her feet. She deserves it." Cashmere responded with a smile.

"I'll be back." Shyla said with a big smile on her face.

Cashmere sat at the table alone, as she took in the beauty of the party. Gold, white and black balloons were everywhere giving her the Hollywood themed feeling. It was gorgeous and the pictures of Skylar all about the place was definitely a reminder of how one should really enjoy life because for some it could be cut short in so little time.

"Hey," a light voice spoke, as the woman seemed to have snuck up on her.

"Hey," Cashmere spoke back with a nervous expression on her face.

"You look good tonight." Tiny said.

"Thanks, so do you." Cashmere responded.

"Well, I just wanted to come over and speak."

Cashmere turned on her fake smile. "Oh ok, nice seeing you again."

"Yea, same here." Tiny said, as she walked off.

The conversation was so brief that it frightened Cashmere, as she nervously sipped her drink. Tiny popping up on her like that scared the shit out of her. She didn't know what the girl had up her sleeves, but she was hoping that she'd mind her own business and stay the hell out of hers.

After scoping the scene once again, she noticed Jabari was nowhere in sight, but that Tiana and Lauren was now seated at a table about to eat. It was so many people in the building it was hard to keep up, but she had to keep Jabari in sight just so she'd know what he was up to at all times. "Where the hell is he?" she mumbled.

"Hey nephew," Jabari said to Cannon, as he reached for him. "You look good as hell tonight." He told Yolanda, as she smiled while handing Cannon over to him.

"Thank you. You look very handsome tonight as well." She told him.

"I didn't know you were going to be here."

"Are you serious? I had to come because I'll be the one leaving with Cannon in about an hour. You know how my sister is. She loves to party and I'm always the babysitter."

"Dang, I feel you though. I appreciate you showing my nephew so much love and attention."

"Well, he is my nephew too." She teased.

"You're right," Jabari said, just as his conversation was interrupted.

"Excuse me, can I talk to you for a second." The guy said.

"Sure," Jabari said.

"Come on Nephew." Yolanda said, as she got Cannon back from Jabari. "We'll be around. Hopefully, I get to see you again before we leave." She told him.

"I'm sure you will. Have fun. Oh, and make sure my mom gets to see him too before you leave."

"Yea, I'm about to take him to Cain now. I don't know where Sofia is at." She said while scoping the crowd, as she walked off.

"Hey, sorry 'bout that. Wassup?" Jabari told the guy, giving him his undivided attention.

The guy held out his hand to shake Jabari's. "Wassup, I'm Leo, Mar's cousin."

Jabari immediately frowned. "Mar's cousin?" he said. "What brings you here tonight?"

"I just came to pay my respects. I know my cousin was in love with your sister once upon a time. So, I'm here paying my respects to her and to him, since he just disappeared off the face of the earth."

"Oh," Jabari said, as he eyed Leo up and down. He didn't know what his motive was, but he didn't trust him one bit. "Why is this the first time we're meeting?"

"Because I don't live around here. I live in California where I was hoping my cousin would join me, but he never showed up. It's been 5 years and I've yet to hear from him."

"Well, I don't think this is the time or the place to discuss that." Jabari told him, as he looked around the party.

"It's not, but I spoke with Slick—"

"Slick?" Jabari pondered with an even more uneasy feeling in his gut. "You talked to Slick, when?"

"When he came out to Cali to visit with some of his people. Nevertheless, this isn't the time or the place to have this conversation, so I'm going to let you get back to your family and guests, but I really want to speak with you again, sooner than later."

"I'd like that too." Jabari told him.

"Here's my card. Call me when you have time. I'll be here for a week before going back."

"A'ight," Jabari said. As Leo walked off, Karen walked up. "Hey Son, your father wants to speak with you and your brothers."

"Now? About what?"

"I don't know, but please go see what he wants. He's down the hall and in the last room on the left." She told him.

"Okay, Ma." Jabari said. The night was getting stranger and stranger. He didn't know what was going on. He looked through the crowd to see Papers and Bruno also heading down the hallway. His frazzled thoughts started traveling in all directions, not knowing what was going on or which way to go. He scanned the crowd again, looking for Leo, but he had seemed to disappear in thin air, kind of similar to his cousin. He shook his head, with an uneasy gut. *What the fuck is going on now?* He pondered to himself.

"Where the hell is your brother?" Biggs asked, as he peeked his head out of the room door.

"I don't know. I figured he'd be right behind me," Justin responded, as he sat down.

"Hell, we've been waiting for about 10 minutes." Papers said. "His slow ass. Probably out there still drinking and dancing."

"Y'all know how Cain is when he gets lit." Jabari uttered. "Bruno you good?"

"Yea," Bruno responded.

"Looks like you've had one too many yourself." Jabari teased.

"I have," Bruno admitted, as Jabari and Justin laughed.

Cain rushed into the room like he knew he was late and about to get chewed out.

"Bout time," Biggs told him. "What was the hold up?"

"Well, um." Cain stuttered. He didn't think it was appropriate for him to tell them that Lauren had hemmed him up in the bathroom and sucked his dick until he oozed down her throat. "Um, I got distracted for a moment. Sorry 'bout that Pops. So, wassup? Why we in here?" he asked, looking from one person to the other.

"Y'all know that Slick's death has been playing heavily on my mind. Not only that, but Skylar's death has also been riding me like a bad nightmare that just won't go away. I honestly feel that the two are connected, and we're gonna get to the bottom of it. It's going to take more than just me and Papers combing the streets because nobody knows nothing, at least that's all we're hearing. So, we have to take a different approach. We need all the resources we can get, even those from Skylar's cold case files."

"I agree." Papers chimed in.

"What you mean, from her cold case files?" Bruno questioned.

"I mean, I'm going to the new lead detective that is over Skylar's case to see what evidence we overlooked. I believe I now know where it lies. I just hope that the resources is there to help us figure this out."

"What resource might that be?" Jabari pondered.

"Skylar was 7 months pregnant, or close to it. I don't believe that baby was Mar's."

"What?" Justin uttered with a confused expression.

"Wow," Jabari whispered.

"Come to think of it, the last conversation we had Skylar said that she had started talking to somebody new. I thought she was only joking, but maybe she was right and that somebody new could've been the baby's real father."

"Yea, but if that was the case then Mars would have probably been the culprit because he was in his feelings." Bruno said.

"But did he know?" Biggs pondered, thinking that Mars never mentioned anything about Skylar's pregnancy the entire time he was being interrogated by him and Papers. "I mean, hell we didn't know. Maybe she didn't tell him. The public didn't even know after her death because we asked to have that information sealed."

"Interesting point." Justin said.

"What's even more interesting is that Mar's cousin Leo is here." Jabari informed them.

Papers frowned. "Is here where and why?" he asked.

"I don't know where he's at now, but he said that he needed to talk with me. I assume it's about Mars. Also, he is the one that spoke with Slick when Slick went out west to visit his family."

"What?" Cain pondered. He'd been so dazed out still thinking about the amazing head that Lauren had just gave him that he wasn't paying much attention. But hearing about Slick talking to Mar's cousin snapped him back to reality.

"Yea, he told me all that. But, we both agreed that this wasn't the time or the place."

"Well, you need to talk with him as soon as possible. I wanna know what this young man has to say about his cousin and why he showed up here to my daughter's celebration."

"Yea nephew, you need to do that asap." Papers said.

"I will," Jabari responded.

"It's something that we're overlooking and whatever that something is will lead us to all the answers we need to know." Papers told them.

"And whatever that is it has something to do with Skylar's pregnancy. I believe that will tell us if Mars was indeed the father. However, I'm starting to have a strong feeling that he wasn't. We never had her baby tested, but there should be samples somewhere that they can test, including Mar's DNA. He was questioned several times. He had to submit his DNA to clear himself, which he passed all tests that were thrown his way, so we're going to use that to see if he really was the father."

"And, if he wasn't?" Bruno asked with a curious expression on his face.

"Then the real father knows more than we think he do." Biggs answered.

"Maybe he didn't want the baby and that's why he killed her. We see this kind of shit all the time on the ID channel." Cain cut in. "Lauren be watching that shit."

Jabari shook his head, as he cut his eyes over at his brother. "The ID channel, Bruh?"

"Yea," Cain responded with serious eyes.

"Well, I guess you got a point." Jabari agreed.

"I'll keep y'all detailed and Jabari the minute you link with Mar's cousin, you let me know. Something is up with that. With him showing up here like that, it's gotta be."

"A'ight Pops, I got you."

"The night is still young, so let's go celebrate Skylar's life. I have a speech to make in about 10 minutes. I don't wanna be late for that or your mom will kill me." He told them.

"Like we need another death on our hands." Cain uttered.

"Really Bruh?" Justin asked with a shake of the head.

"I'm just saying." Cain shrugged.

"Well, I have a hot date that's waiting on me. So, I'm out." Justin said, as he was first to exit the room.

"Pops your grandson and granddaughter are out there for a little while."

Biggs smiled. "Make sure I see them tonight before they leave."

"Oh, I will." Cain assured him. "Ma had Cannon by the time I was heading in here. I hope my daughter is still out there somewhere. Her mom don't be playing around. I was glad she showed up though."

"Yea, make sure I meet her too before they leave." Jabari said. "Well, I need to go check on Cash. She had her lips poked out earlier."

"I saw that," Cain cut in. "She didn't like you escorting Tiana in here."

"I know, but she'll be alright." Jabari said, as he left the room with Cain following him.

Bruno sat back sipping from his straight Hennessy with all types of thoughts running through his mind. He quietly watched as Biggs and Papers left the room. Talking about Skylar always did something to him. He had mad love for her in more ways than any of the family knew and it broke his heart to know that she'd left this earth in such a tragic way. He stared out the window and up into the sky. "Damn, Skylar I miss you." He couldn't help but reminisce about the last time they were together.

"You missed me?" Skylar asked, as she entered the trailer that she and Bruno always met in. She wasted no time walking over and giving him the biggest hug ever.

He kissed her softly on the lips. "Hell yea, I missed you. Where you been? You're like an hour late." He said, looking at his watch.

"I know. I had to talk with Mom and Pops."

"How did that go? I hope you didn't mention that we were skipping town tomorrow."

"Hell no. I did tell my brothers though. Well, Justin and Jabari."

"Why would you do that?" Bruno pondered with a frown on his face.

"I didn't tell them with who. I just said that I was leaving town." She explained.

"Damn babe. I hate you did that. I wish you would've waited."

"I'm actually glad I didn't because talking to them allowed me to come to my senses."

"What you mean by that?"

"Well," she said while walking off and fidgeting with her hands. "You're really not going to like this."

"What?" Bruno anxiously pondered.

"I told Justin and Jabari that I was pregnant."

"What?!" Bruno said, as he began to pace back and forth. "You can't do that right now."

"Well, I did." Skylar told him. "I also told my parents."

Bruno shot Skylar a mean stare. "Are you fucking kidding me?!"

"Babe calm down. They were going to find out anyway."

"And, when they did we'd be far away." He told her.

By: Tiece

"Listen at yourself. I'll be turning 19 in a few hours; you're fucking 33 years old. You should know better. I don't wanna leave my family and I don't wanna have my baby and they can't be a part of her life. You've been putting so much pressure on me to keep our relationship hidden and it's not fair anymore. I have to be honest with them about everything. Maybe not about you right now, but eventually the truth will come out."

"You don't understand. We've been fucking around since you were 16. If your father and your uncle knew that they'd have me killed."

"You're being dramatic. I'm grown now."

"Yea, but it's the principle. That can never come out."

"So, what were you thinking? We were just going to move, and I'd never come back? I mean, I know I say crazy shit when I'm mad, but I would never leave my family for good."

Bruno stood at the window looking out of it. He didn't know what to think. His brilliant idea wasn't so brilliant at all. He really didn't know what he was thinking besides not being killed by Skylar's father.

"I'm sorry." He told her, as he walked over and gave her a hug. "I didn't mean to pressure you. I know you've been doing things for years that clearly you didn't want to do. Like leading Mars on to throw your parents off my tracks."

"Yea, and we've been doing that so long till I don't know what's real and what's not." She told him. "Hell, sometimes I think I even confuse him."

"But you're not confused about this baby are you?"

"No, I know who my child's father is." She told him.

"You better." He teased. "You're going to eventually have to tell Mars the truth, though."

"That would include telling him everything. You ready for that, because he's gonna tell it. Especially when he learns I'm pregnant and it's not by him. Plus, have you told your wife yet?"

"I was planning on leaving with you, so what does that tell you?"

"That just tells me that you were leaving with me. It don't say nothing about you telling your wife shit."

"Don't start Skylar."

"I'm just saying. So, that's on you. If you wanna keep playing these games then I'll keep playing them too. Which means that Mars will pass as being my daughter's father."

"You must be foolish. That ain't gon' happen!"

"Well, you better figure something out and you got until tomorrow to do so."

"Are you serious?"

"Hell yea, I'm serious." She told him. "I can't keep doing this. I wanna start a family of my own and I'd prefer it be with you, but if you can't bring this relationship out to the world, then I'm out of it. Me and my baby," she told him with a serious stare.

"So, you're giving me an ultimatum?"

"Yep," she said. "I am."

"You're willing to risk my life?"

"Yep, to live mine peacefully." She answered. "They don't have to know that we've been fucking around since I was 16. We could always tell them that we started seeing each other when I was 18."

"You really think that's gon' make a difference? You're still his baby girl and I'm still a married, grown ass man."

"Well, babe I don't know what to tell you. The choice is yours." She said, while looking down at her watch. "I can't keep living like this."

Bruno stood there for a minute. He loved Skylar. Unfortunately, he wasn't ready for her parents or nobody else to know. However, he knew he couldn't keep her from living the life she deserved, but he didn't feel that Mars was right for her either.

"I want you to be happy and I wish it could be with me, but nobody can ever know that we were together. I have too much to lose."

"Wow," Skyla uttered. "It's like that?"

"It has to be." Bruno told her. "I guess you're going to keep up this charade with Mars?"

"No, I'm telling Mars it's over tonight. As a matter of fact, he's supposed to meet me out here?"

"Out here?"

"Yea."

"Damn, Skylar! You doing too much! What if that nigga pulls up and I'm out here?"

"Well, you better leave then." She said, with her hand on her hip. "You better be glad I have compassion for your situation, or I would out your ass myself. You've played with my emotions long enough. You never wanted my parents to know about you and that's fucked up. I mean, I can understand you not wanting them to know back when we first started fucking around, but damn I'm grown now. If you were gonna be like this, you should've told me, and I could've been shook you out my system. I don't even believe you were ever leaving your wife! Was that all a lie too just to get me away from my people so you could control the situation?"

"I don't wanna hear this right now."

"I bet you don't. The only time we're good is when I'm doing what you want me to do. The only time we're not arguing is when we're having sex. You've played with my mental long enough and I'm over it."

By: Tiece

"Fine time for you to say that now that you're pregnant."

"Whatever," Skylar said, and as Bruno attempted to walk out she hauled off and busted him in the back of the head with her fist. "You dirty muthafucka! You basically used me and now I'm pregnant with your baby and you wanna walk out and leave me."

"You don't know who the fucking father is. Don't kid me. You were fucking Mars too."

"And, you were still fucking your wife!" she yelled, slapping him across the face.

Bruno reached back to hit her but caught himself.

"Yea hit me. I'll make sure my father knows about us."

"You threatening me?"

"Yep," Skylar said.

"Babe, are you coming to party with me or not?" Bruno's wife asked, as she entered the room, interrupting his thoughts. "Biggs told me you were in here."

Bruno cleared his throat. "Yea, I'm coming."

"You alright?"

"Yea, I'm good." He answered, but he wasn't good. He wasn't good at all. It was way too much going on for him to stay focused, but he had to get a grip and figure out his next move, because if he didn't think it out carefully, it could be his last.

Jabari sat at the bar, waiting for him and Tiana's drink. He noticed Bruno and his wife heading out on the dance floor. For some reason, Bruno's whole demeanor had been off and it all started around the time Slick was killed. Although, he felt it impossible for Bruno to have something to do with Slick's death, he still couldn't help but wonder. Everybody was now suspect, including members of the crew that his father trusted. Besides blood, no one was to be trusted and Bruno was numeral Uno on his list. He needed to know what was really going on with him and the sooner the better.

"Hey, Jabari," a light voice said from behind.

"Hey Tiny." Jabari said, as he turned to face her. "How are you? I'm glad to see that you came out tonight."

"Yea, I wouldn't have missed it for the world." She said.

"You want me to order you a drink?"

Tiny held up her glass. "Nah, this is like my second one already. I need to pace myself." She grinned.

"I feel you. So, what's up? The last time we saw each other you acted like you had something you wanted to get off your chest."

"Yea, I kind of did and I guess right now wouldn't be the best of timing to tell you. I did stop by your parents' house, but you weren't there. I left my number with your mom to call me, but you never did." She said.

"I'm sure she forgot to tell me. She be having so much on her mind. Sorry 'bout that. But, you good? What'd you need to talk with me about?" *Oh God*, Jabari thought just as he spotted Cashmere eyeing him down from across the room.

"Well, what I wanted to say I really couldn't at the doctor's office. Not while your girl was there," she said.

"Who? Cashmere?" he frowned.

"Yea."

"And, why is that?" he asked, just as he could see Cashmere heading his way.

"Because that baby might not be yours."

Jabari frowned with an uncertain expression on his face. "Say what now?" he asked.

"I said—"

"Heyyy, so we meet again," Cashmere butted in, as she walked up invading their conversation.

"Heyyy," Tiny nervously smiled. She looked at Jabari with an uneasy expression on her face.

"I'm not interrupting anything important am I?" Cashmere asked.

"No," Tiny quickly answered, and then looked over at Jabari. "We'll catch up later. I ain't going nowhere."

Jabari nodded his head as an indication that it was cool for her to walk off, but he stared at Cashmere with bothered eyes.

"You good? You a'ight?" Cashmere asked, trying not to show how concerned she really was.

"Yea," Jabari told her. He had no plans to make the night any worse by bringing up what Tiny had just said. However, he couldn't take his mind off it. What could Tiny be talking about and how would she possibly know anything about Cashmere besides her once being his lady? He shook his head with uneasy thoughts, as the bartender bought over his drinks.

"Well, I know that ain't for me." Cashmere joked.

By: Tiece

"Nah, it's not. But hey, I hope you're enjoying yourself. I'll catch up with you later." He told her and just like that, he walked off. Now wasn't the time for him to go into details that even he was unsure about, but one thing was for sure. Every dog had its day, and Cashmere's was coming. What she didn't know was that it would be sooner than later if she was lying to him about the baby she was carrying. Only time or the truth would tell, and he was hell bent on getting to the bottom of everything that could compromise his happiness or his freedom.

To Be Continued...

Other Books Written by Tiece...

*Falling In Love With The Goat 1-3 (Complete Series)
*Just Can't Leave Him Alone 1-5, Originally Titled, CheckMate (Complete Series)
*I Need Love 1-4, Originally Titled, SCARLETT (Complete Series)
*Drunk in Love 1-4 (Also Available In a Complete Box-set)
*Woman To Woman 1-3 (Also Available in a Complete box-set)
*The First Wife 1-3
*Shanice Capone's Truth, A Shorty Story (Located at the end of The First Wife part 3)
*Classy & Ratchet, Originally Titled, Ratchet Bitches 1-2
*Southern Gossip 1-2
*It's Either Me Or Her 1-2
*A Boss Valentine In Atlanta (A Short Story)
*These Games We Play 1
*Dopeboyz & the Women That Love 'em
*My Girl Got a Girlfriend 1-2 (Turned into A Standalone Novel)
*Shorty Found Love With a Dope Boy, Originally Titled, Thug Lovin' Is The Best Lovin' 1-2 (Turned into A Standalone Novel)
*For The Love Of My Trap King 1-2 Originally Titled, Shawty Is My Rock (A completed Series, Will be turned into a Standalone Novel)

www.ingramcontent.com/pod-product-compliance
Lightning Source LLC
Chambersburg PA
CBHW062217150726
47991CB00006B/2324